CHARIS

JOURNEY TO PANDORA'S JAR

NICOLE Y. WALTERS

booktrope

Booktrope Editions
Seattle WA 2013

Illustrations & Cover Design
by Vincent Andrew Conard

Edited by Dawn Pearson

This is a work of fiction. Names, characters, places, brands, media, and incidents are either the product of the author's imagination or are used fictitiously. Any resemblance to similarly named places or to persons living or deceased is unintentional.

PRINT ISBN 978-1-62015-134-1
EPUB ISBN 978-1-62015-109-9

For further information regarding permissions, please contact info@booktrope.com.

Library of Congress Control Number: 2013938695

For Marc, Ryan, and Cole—
Thank you for constantly believing in good, in love, and in hope.
And thank you for not only believing in those most noble ideals,
but for living them too.
I love you.

For Mom and Dad—
You first opened my eyes to wonder.

SUNDAY NIGHT

Great deeds are usually wrought at great risks.

—HERODOTUS

CHAPTER 1
A BLACKER BLACK,
A WARMER WARM

HAD MR. WARD BEEN PAYING closer attention when he walked into Storage Room 19, he might have noticed that the warm was just a little bit warmer and the black was just a little bit blacker than usual. That he didn't notice those small yet horribly significant details was unusual. The exactly matched blue of his tie, belt, and his shoes and socks betrayed his love for details, details, details; a talent that served him well as museum curator.

It was his appreciation for the particulars that brought him to the storage room in the first place. He couldn't understand how he had missed such an obvious mistake on the inventory sheet, and for such an important occasion. Friday night was the start of *The Ancients Alive,* a Greek antiquities exhibition. He was sure he had checked and double-checked each item. Yet here he stood, flustered, looking for an additional, missing crate.

Mr. Ward adjusted the smart-looking spectacles on his narrow nose for the millionth time. His jaws clenched as he stared down at the inventory sheet, waiting for the mysterious item to magically disappear in the same way it had appeared. When he was sure that wouldn't happen, he climbed his pencil-thin body up, then down, the ladder, scanning every shelf. Mr. Ward stood in the middle of the room with his hands on his hips, tapping his wingtip shoes.

"If it was a snake, it would have bitten me by now," he grumbled aloud.

The tired fellow removed his glasses, rubbed his eyes, and then replaced them on his nose where they promptly slid right back down. Mr. Ward took a deep breath as he resigned himself to search every blasted nook and cranny *again*. He felt foolish making the effort though. He didn't expect the crate to contain anything very special at all. Its inventory information was horribly incomplete. It said nothing about where the crate came from, who had received it into the museum, or even the name of the object inside it. It simply read: "Jar and Cover, Ancient Greek."

He shook his head and ran his fingers through his receding blond hair.

"Shoddy work. Shoddy work indeed," he muttered, making a mental note to chew out whoever was responsible. Mr. Ward loosened his perfectly coordinated tie, noticing the warmer warm for the first time.

"That's another thing I'll report. Everyone *knows* the temperature in these rooms needs to be carefully regulated," he said to no one.

Mr. Ward wiped beads of sweat from his brow and walked toward the air-conditioner controls. On the way, the inventory sheet slipped out of his sweaty fingers and drifted beneath one of the bottom shelves.

"Goodness gracious," he huffed, easing himself down on one knee to search for the paper. "What in heaven's name?"

The linoleum was warm against Mr. Ward's stomach as he lay on the ground, adjusted his glasses, and squinted into the blacker black beneath the shelf. There, in the dark recess, sat the missing crate. It was cloaked, rather intentionally it seemed, by the darkness around it.

"Well, I'll be …" he exclaimed, reaching out his spindly arm.

'Well, I'll be' was the last thing Mr. Ward said before the deep growl, violent jerking, flash of light, and deafening sucking sound snatched him away. His scream, piercing. His struggle, brief. His disappearance, final.

Gone was Mr. Ward with his perfectly matched wardrobe and ill-fitting glasses.

Gone was the warm that was just a little bit warmer, and the black that was just a little bit blacker.

Gone.

Only the mysterious crate remained.

MONDAY

The only true wisdom is in knowing you know nothing.

—SOCRATES

CHAPTER 2
STRANGE DREAMS AND WINGED THINGS

THE DREAMS INTERRUPTING Charis's sleep were pretty much the same every night. For the past couple of weeks, as soon as she closed her eyes they'd begin. She found herself standing in a great, golden room, so big that every sound she made echoed and bounced off the walls. When the dreams first started, she'd yell "Hey" or "Anybody there?" just because she got a kick out of hearing it over and over again. Now, she couldn't wait to get this part of the dream over with to see if maybe, just maybe, she could finally get to the dream's end.

Eventually, her feet—pointed and with her nails painted a soft blue—would float above the smooth, marble surface beneath them as she drifted down the familiar hall. Floods of opaque, yellow light came from everywhere, including her own skin, and filled the halls of what Charis had come to believe was a palace or museum of some sort. She'd squint her eyes as she studied her illuminated hands, arms, and feet, intrigued.

Charis would continue floating down the wide corridor toward somewhere she suspected was important. On the way, she'd stop to admire the paintings that decorated the shining walls. They were unlike anything she'd ever seen in real life. These paintings were animated and absolutely alive with color and movement; each brushstroke contained a measure of magic. From within beautiful gilded frames, the crashing waves of the ocean sprayed the girl with salt water, roaring lions in caves startled her as she drifted by, and instruments played music from invisible hands that she danced to with an equally invisible partner.

Charis loved all of the paintings, but her favorites were the portraits. The proud man with the curly hair man was the most handsome fellow Charis had ever seen, but she didn't blush until she happened upon the kissing lovers whose passion she found shocking. And, even though she knew none of this was real, Charis's eyes welled with tears gazing upon the wounded warrior staring helplessly back at her from a bloodied battlefield. These were just a few of the many curious portraits lining the walls.

As Charis watched, the men and women in the pictures attempted to talk with her. Try as she might, she couldn't understand a word they said. For all of their babble, they may as well have been the bleating sheep or singing birds from the other paintings. Still, they did their best to communicate. What, Charis couldn't tell. Some threw her flowers and danced and bowed in her presence as though she were a god or they her royal subjects. Others, characters of the darker sort, hissed at her and yelled what Charis guessed were curses. She didn't like them.

It wasn't long before all of the portraits yelled together and got louder and louder until Charis couldn't take it anymore. "Calm down," she'd say, but they just kept right on yelling and making her nervous. It was usually then—with her hands over her ears to mute the noise—that Charis woke up, tired, groggy, and a little confused, just like this morning.

With the memory of her dream still clinging to her lashes like oil, Charis opened her brown eyes. She untangled herself from her bed sheets and rolled onto her back, determined to remember more of the dream this time. Snapshots of beautiful faces and bright, flooding light drifted just beyond her remembrance and vanished before she could see any of it clearly. It was so real, but she just couldn't grab it and it drove her nuts. She hated starting mornings with such frustration. Here lately, it had been *every* morning.

Forget it. She kicked away her covers and stretched her lanky body across the bed, yawning.

"Charis?" Mona called from the bottom of the stairs. "You up?"

"Yes, Mom," she answered, her voice full of morning gravel.

"Well, you'd better get a move on, sweetie. You know you have that test today, so give yourself time for breakfast, okay?"

"M'kay."

God, it's going to be a long day, Charis thought. A sleepless night was bad enough, but there was Mr. Porter's algebra test too. She and Gabe had studied for hours over popcorn and Gatorade. Now that the day of the test was here, she wondered if they'd studied enough and she regretted all of the Facebooking they'd done in between. Her current status? Nervous.

"Too late now," she sighed.

She scratched her head, her fingers becoming lost in mess of her sandy curls, and rolled out of bed for a shower. Standing beneath the warm water, Charis decided not to freak out about the test and ran through formulas in her head instead. *You've got this. It's just like breathing* she thought while filling her lungs with shower steam. When she was done, she drip-dropped her way to the sink and squeezed the water from her hair. It drew back into its clumsy spirals before she even finished.

Charis stared intensely into the steamy mirror before lifting her finger to write 'prepared' in the moisture on the glass. She added a question mark as an afterthought but quickly erased it. Bad luck. She stepped back to read her work, satisfied, and watched it slowly disappear before heading to her room to dress.

Charis threw on some jeans and her favorite sweater and went downstairs for breakfast. Her parents were talking and having coffee at the kitchen table, solving the world's problems. Charis's parents met in college. Their romance was fairly typical, except that Evan was white and Mona was black. It wasn't a big deal to them, but it was to their families. Fortunately for the couple, love prevailed and their families got over it, mostly. Aunt Diane was still a holdout at family gatherings but no one really cared that much. She was weird about a lot of things, and had too many cats anyway.

"Morning, Sunny," Evan said looking up from his laptop, his blue eyes shining at her. He was such a morning person. "You ready?"

Charis hugged him around his neck and hoped she'd smell like his cologne all day. She loved her daddy.

"I'm always ready, Dad. You know that!"

She sounded more confident than she felt. Charis grabbed a cereal bowl while her mom got the milk from the fridge.

"Mr. Porter said this will be the hardest test so far, but I think I got it. Me and Gabe ..."

"Gabe and I," corrected Mona, raising one perfectly arched eyebrow.

"*Gabe and I* studied really hard for this one. It's like 50% of our grade or something like that."

"You just be sure algebra is the only thing Gabe is studying," Evan responded.

Charis rolled her eyes. "Daaaad, it's not like that."

"I've seen the way that boy acts when he's over here ... all left feet. It's a wonder he can dribble a basketball without falling over himself."

Evan got up from the kitchen table for more coffee. He gave his best Gabe impression as he poured his second cup.

"'Uh, h~h~hello Mr. Mr. Parks. How was your d~d~day, Mr. Mr. Parks?'" Evan laughed. "He's over here so much I'm going to start claiming that kid on my income taxes."

Charis had to admit it. Whenever Gabe was near her dad the boy couldn't seem to get his words out. It wasn't like he was the coolest kid in school or anything, but he was downright goofy around her father.

Charis first met Gabe in the third grade. They sat next to each other in Mrs. Cole's class. It started off badly between them on the very first day. There was a cursive writing test and, in short, Charis's was a mess, and Gabe's a work of elementary school art.

"Charis, look at Gabe's handwriting," Mrs. Cole beamed standing over the two of them. "Isn't it just beautiful? You should try to write like that. I'm sure Gabe will help you. Won't you Gabe?"

Gabe puffed out his scrawny chest and smiled down at Charis. Her face burned red with a mix of embarrassment, anger, and jealousy. She could plainly see that Gabe's writing was better than hers and didn't need Mrs. Cole or Gabe to point out the obvious. Charis looked at Gabe's buck-toothed grin, swallowed her pride, and mumbled, "Good job Gabe." His pompous, jerky smirk melted away, and with his *own* face now a bright red, Gabe offered to help Charis if she wanted. They formed a truce and from then on they were best buds.

When Gabe's mom took off and his parents divorced last year, he started hanging out more at Charis's house for the company. His own home was too quiet and sad and full of cardboard-tasting frozen dinners. He and Charis did homework or played Xbox together while he and Mr. Parks fought over the last fried chicken leg.

Evan continued, "For someone as tall and skinny as he is, that boy manages to eat up everything in this house. I don't know where it all goes ..."

Charis and her mom both shook their heads. They'd heard it all before.

"Where's Presley?" Charis asked her mom, hoping to change the subject.

"He left early this morning. *Driving lessons.*" Mona said it like she was narrating one of those old black and white horror movies where the bad guys wore thick white makeup and slicked back hair and the women stood around screaming instead of running.

Presley was Charis's older brother. He would be sixteen years old in a few weeks and driving was all he could talk about. His excitement was a departure from his usual cool. Previous attempts by Evan and Mona to teach Presley how to drive always ended up with swearing and promises to never, *ever* give him the keys again. So, for the sake of the family, they decided to put him in driving school. Presley was glad to go. Either way, Charis couldn't wait for her brother to get his driver's license. Two words: personal chauffeur.

Charis put her bowl in the dishwasher and grabbed her backpack to leave. Gabe would be there any minute for their walk to school.

"Ugh" she said as she swung the bulging pink bag over her shoulders.

Mona looked at her with concern. "What's wrong, babe?"

"I've been meaning to tell you ... my birthmark, it's been itching again. It's just a little tender, that's all."

"Charis, now you know I've asked you to tell me if ..."

"I know, I know." She winced as she adjusted the backpack on her shoulders.

When Charis was born the first thing the doctor said was, "Look, you have yourselves a little angel." It wasn't because she was so cute (though her mom and dad certainly thought so); it was because of the small birthmark between her shoulder blades. It was shaped, nearly perfectly, like a little pair of pale wings. As she stretched and grew, so did her wings. Through the years doctors assured her parents it was nothing to worry about. However, they advised them to keep an eye on it just the same. And so they did. They also mused about the fact that their cherub-faced baby girl had wings.

Charis may have been as cute as an angel, but she didn't always behave like one. Ever since she was a child, the girl had been just a little headstrong. At least that's what her parents called it. It was more complicated than that to Charis. She just wanted to know the reasons why, perhaps a bit more than most kids.

By the time she was five years old, it was clear to her parents that they could take nothing for granted with their girl. Whether it was deciding on what clothes to wear, or explaining what motivated God to flood the very earth he created, Charis needed to know why. Why? Why? Why? If they couldn't answer her, then she demanded that her teachers did. If they couldn't, then her pastor, or librarian, or the neighbor up the street. It could go on forever. This troubled Charis's parents who mistook her questions for something more than just curiosity. So, instead of entertaining their daughter with angelic tales about winged creatures such as herself, they told her cautionary ones. A favorite was the Greek myth of Icarus.

Outfitted with new wings made of wax and feathers, Icarus ignored his father's warning not to fly too close to the sun during their escape from the island of Crete. Enthralled by the adventure and lured by his own curiosity, Icarus didn't listen to his father and flew higher and higher until the sun's heat melted the wax on his feathers and destroyed his wings. The curious boy tumbled from the sky and into the sea where he drowned.

When Charis was slow to listen to her parents' instructions and behaved irresponsibly like Icarus during his flight toward the sun, Evan and Mona would say things like, "You're getting awfully sunny there, Charis." Those warnings were issued so often that Sunny eventually became Charis's nickname. To the surprise of her parents, Charis's constant questioning lessened as she matured, but that was mostly due to peer pressure. Her friends found it annoying too and didn't hesitate to say so.

"I'll make an appointment with Dr. Nuu." Mona said.

"No, Mom. Don't worry about it. It's okay, I promise," Charis replied as the doorbell announcing Gabe rang.

"Gabe is here," Evan sang as he jingled his keys, preparing to leave. *Keys!*

Charis ran upstairs to get the unusual trinket she had found in her backpack. It was a beautiful crystal fairy-like thing that glowed in jewel tones in just the right light. She noticed it at the bottom of her backpack Sunday while doing her homework. *I bet Gabe put you in there, didn't he?* she thought as she traced the grooves of its etched wings with her fingernails. The doll had long hair and a tiny sword that hung from its waist. Charis ended up attaching it to a key ring and claimed it as her own.

"There you are," she said picking it up from the nightstand and clipping it to her jeans.

Ding-dong.

"Coming!"

Charis charged down the stairs and ran into the kitchen to kiss her mom and dad goodbye before sliding across the wood floors toward the front door. When she opened it, there was Gabe, all left feet and goofy, just like her dad said.

CHAPTER 3
THE PROBLEM WITH HADES

IT WAS MORE OF A ROAR than a question. His voice rang out like a clash of cymbals over the constant moaning in the background. The words sprang from his mouth like punches and echoed on the glistening gray, stone walls.

"Tell me again," Hades bellowed. "What is your pitiful excuse?"

He leaned his body forward in the seat of his elaborate throne. It was decorated with the bones of men and blackened with soot. The gaze of his black eyes bore into the space where Megaera's eyes would have been if she were not made almost entirely of smoke. Hades's goal was to intimidate. He was good at that.

Megaera's shadowy, winged figure stood defiantly erect before him, but she did bow her head as a courtesy. She wasn't stupid. This was Hades, and it wasn't wise to provoke him unnecessarily. She had already made such a grave, costly error.

"No excuse, *friend*. Just the truth," she hissed along with the snakes upon her head. "The truth is all I have."

Megaera waved a withered hand, and the word 'truth' appeared in the air, a sickly green. The word floated up and hovered before Hades as if awaiting his acknowledgement.

"You also greet me empty-handed!" he stormed. Hades slapped his hefty hand against his armrest and caused 'truth' to airily vanish away. The anger on his face betrayed its usual handsome calm. He threw his pewter-colored body back onto his throne and let out a frustrated sigh.

"Tell me … again … what happened. And slowly this time. I want to try and make some sense of your failure."

Hades peered into her blackened face, what he could make of it. He would be careful with his anger, temper it with wisdom. He knew that the relationship he shared with Megaera was a tricky one. He needed her and her wretched sisters.

The Erinyes Sisters—Megaera, Tisiphone, and Alecto—had served his kingdom well throughout the ages. As the avengers of wrongs, they dragged guilty men and women before Hades with relish, many still screaming their last living cries of horror. Hades would then dispense the punishment their crimes deserved. It was what he did. Yes, he needed the Erinyes Sisters, and the morbid, underhanded work they performed for him. A devious smile crossed his face because he knew they needed him too.

Without him, the snake-haired, red-eyed, black-winged sisters were useless. He was the only thing standing between them and the threat of obscurity. Given their unpleasant work, they hadn't many friends on Mt. Olympus. The other gods hardly acknowledged their existence. Still, the agreement Hades shared with them was an uneasy one, symbiotic though it was. Individually, the Erinyes Sisters were difficult to manage. Dealing with them all *together* gave Hades an unholy headache.

"As I've told you before, my Lord," Megaera said, carefully. "I located the object of your desire, but before I could bring it back into your benevolent arms, the 'problem' arose."

As she spoke, a loud moan also arose from somewhere in the blacker black behind her. Megaera rolled her eyes within her shadowy face. She needn't be reminded of her failure at the museum.

"Quiet," she yelled. "Quiet" flew from her mouth in red and dove into the darkness toward the moan. Silence resulted.

"This unexpected 'problem' interrupted our mission, and so I had to abort it, to protect it, me … to protect you."

There was a long, uncomfortable silence signaling a reluctant agreement.

"The object of your desire remains hidden, unknown to anyone else, save you and me. To all else, it is unknown."

Megaera's shadowy silhouette bowed, deeply this time. She was done with her explanation. It would have to be enough. It was the truth. Countless years of listening to groveling humans trying to explain away the evil they'd done had taught the Erinyes Sisters one thing—neither opinions, nor feelings, nor intentions mattered in the end. Only the truth did.

"This is the truth," she reminded herself and Hades.

At this, the gray god felt some relief. At least they knew where the jar, the "object of his affection" was, and that it was still hidden. Apparently, all was *not* lost in spite of the ineptitude of his helper, who he thought stood too proudly before him. He would remember her arrogance in the future and wisely wondered if it was a family trait she shared with her sisters.

Foolish Erinyes Sisters.

Hades needed another plan to get the jar back, but he had to be careful and not attract too much attention from the gods … or the humans. He would be patient, for now, and let the Erinyes Sisters continue to do the dirty work and take the risks.

When he was finished staring down Megaera, Hades turned his gaze toward the pathetic, skinny man cowering shamelessly in the corner behind her. The red word 'quiet' was pressed over his mouth just beneath his crooked glasses.

"And what do you, Megaera, suggest we do with this *problem*?" Hades asked, nodding toward Mr. Ward.

Looking over her shoulder with beady, red eyes hardly visible to Hades or the unfortunate curator, Megaera chortled. "I'm sure Sisyphus would appreciate help rolling his boulder up the hill, my Lord Hades. Some help for Sisyphus and his boulder."

Poor Mr. Ward shrunk deeper into the fetal position and shivered wildly against the wet floor.

CHAPTER 4
MEAN GIRLS AND MYTHOLOGY

THE BELL ENDING FIRST PERIOD rang out and so did the sighs of relief from Mr. Porter's algebra students. As promised, the test was hard. Charis and Gabe hustled out of the classroom and into the school's open hallways. They huddled together, anxious to compare answers. Loud kids hurried past them as they walked slowly, doing a mental review.

"I know I got the last question wrong," Gabe said. "And, not because I ran out of time, either."

Gabe had the habit of running a hand over his head whenever he was nervous. His hair stood up in every which way right now.

"If I had all day I *still* couldn't solve that thing," he admitted.

Charis put on her jacket against the mild December breeze. She kept it to herself that not only was she able to answer the last question, but she finished the extra credit one too. Gabe still had better handwriting than she did, but Charis had the edge with math.

Andrea, the third musketeer of their group, startled Charis and Gabe when she ran up behind them. She didn't say a word. She just stood there, waving her hands up and down frantically like she was trying to fly. This was her "excited" move. She had several others.

"Hey, Andy," Gabe said, knowing he'd be ignored.

"Oh my God! Oh my God! Oh my God!" Andy squealed. "Charis! I just heard that Brady asked Lauren to the Jolly Jam dance on Friday. Lauren!"

Andy covered her mouth with her hands. It was the only way she would stay quiet long enough for Charis to say something. Charis loved Andy, but she had a big mouth, and it was usually full of gossip just like this. About Brady and Lauren: if middle school had kings and queens, then those two would definitely wear the crowns. If not the *center* of the 'it' crowd, they were easily VIP members.

"Of course he did … I mean, I figured as much. They hang out all the time," Charis said, as if it wasn't a big deal. But it was, even if only to her. She wasn't exactly the party girl type, and was definitely more comfortable in jeans than dresses, but she couldn't imagine anyone, including herself, turning down an invitation from Brady. In fact, she'd imagined many times how she would say yes if he asked her.

"I know you wanted to go with him, Charis," Andy said.

"Huh?" Charis felt her face go flushed. "What makes you say that?"

"Well, in case you haven't noticed, you've been doing a lot of 'Brady this' and 'Brady that' lately."

Charis hadn't noticed, but Andy apparently did. Charis had to admit that she felt some chemistry with Brady since working together in English class on the play. She felt butterflies in her stomach and everything, and had let herself imagine Brady felt it too. After all, he was the one who kept going on and on about how happy he was to be in her group. Charis assumed that just maybe …

"You can't go to the dance anyway," Gabe interrupted, sounding a little too happy about it. "Friday night is the tour of the museum, remember?"

"Yeah, that's right. The tour," Charis repeated.

The J. Paul Getty Museum in Los Angeles was about to launch its *The Ancients Alive* exhibition featuring Greek gods and goddesses. Charis's mom's advertising firm had landed the Getty account and the entire agency had been invited to attend the exclusive preview party event. Like Charis, Gabe loved Greek mythology, so she had invited him along.

"Still," Andy finally said, rolling her eyes and neck. "Lauren? He could do better."

Charis agreed. Lauren was just so … so …

"What's up, Charis?"

So *right* in her face.

"Oh, hey Lauren," Charis said, taking a step back … or trying to at least. She couldn't move with Lauren's adoring fans surrounding her on all sides. Without fail, a group of around six girls traveled with Lauren wherever she went, hovering and waiting for the chance to serve Her Highness.

"Not much. What's up with you?" Charis said. She watched with a smidgen of envy as Lauren twisted a lock of her silky, cooperative, straight blonde hair around her finger. She wondered what her own wild mane was doing at the moment. Charis swore Lauren must have read her mind because the girl let out a small chuckle as a lock of Charis's wayward hair decided to dangle across her eyes. Charis cursed the ill-timed gust of wind and shoved her hair behind her ears.

"Not much. Just the dance. Friday. With Brady … but I'm sure you know that already, doesn't she, *Andrea*?"

Lauren cut her eyes at Andy who suddenly took a keen interest in the cement beneath her feet. For once in her life, Andy was content to be quiet.

"What are *you* doing Friday?" Lauren asked, turning her piercing blue eyes from Andy back to Charis. The look on Lauren's perfect face was more bored than interested.

"Nothing special," Charis mumbled.

"Awwww," Lauren said with pouty pink lips. "Of course not. Just another Friday night, huh?" Charis heard snickering behind her.

Lauren's mission of humiliation complete, she sang, "Well, tootles" and skipped off to class with her loyal subjects strutting behind.

Charis rolled her eyes. Of course after Lauren left she realized she could have told Miss Perfect about her plans at the Getty and how instead of dancing with Brady she'd be enjoying an evening full of history, myth, and legend. That was way more important than some silly middle school dance with the boy of her dreams anyway.

Nothing special … what tha?

She thought back to the bathroom mirror this morning. Her word was "prepared." Stinging from the vacuous exchange with Lauren, Charis realized algebra wasn't the only thing she should have been prepared for. Embarrassment washed her face. It must have been obvious because Gabe reached out to hold Charis's hand before thinking better of it and shoving his own in his pockets instead.

"She's such a pompous moron! Let's go," Andy said, suddenly finding her voice *and* courage in Lauren's absence.

"Yeah, let's," Charis sighed.

At least she had English class to look forward to. She loved it, especially now that they were studying Greek mythology and she could let her imagination run wild with Athena, Poseidon, Zeus ... and Brady, dance or not.

CHAPTER 5
THE PLIGHT AND FLIGHT
OF HERMES

EVEN IF THEY DIDN'T HAVE WINGS on them, Hermes's feet still wouldn't have touched the ground as happy as he was. Happy and relieved. The bright sunlight and gentle breeze gracing Mt. Olympus matched his mood perfectly.

As the Messenger God, Hermes was always *giving* news.

> *"There is a war threatening to erupt between China and North Korea."*
> *"The United States is on the verve of an epic financial crisis."*
> *"South Africa is breaking out in civil unrest."*

On and on it went. The news Hermes carried constantly sent gods and goddesses secretly flying in and out of human affairs. They did what they could to avert sure disaster, while risking their own exposure and safety in the process. It was a nasty job that often went unappreciated and unnoticed.

Man.

Lately, it seemed the news Hermes delivered was getting progressively worse, and more and more frequent. So, receiving a bit of good news every now and then was nice. Like now. In spite of the close call at the museum last night, the crate with the jar was still safe. Hermes shook his head as he thought about Megaera almost ruining everything. The pathetic creature almost captured the jar.

Outcast!

The air around Hermes grew thick and heavy, like his thoughts. That is how it was with Hermes. When his mood changed, so did the atmosphere. It was an effective way to deliver messages—they were both heard and felt, ensuring that what he had to say was understood loud and clear.

It had been Hermes's idea for Ericthonious to place the jar among the other crates at the museum. It was easier for him to do it. He was a demigod and could disguise himself as human more easily than the gods could. Hermes knew that if everything went as planned, the Grace would eventually find the jar. It was the best plan he could muster—nearly perfect, or so he thought. Hermes had not considered how soon Hades would notice it missing after he stole it from him.

"Not 'stole'," he said aloud to himself, his voice rich and plush like velvet. "I *relocated* it to a more proper place." Hermes tossed his silver hair out of his icy blue eyes.

Hades! What was he doing with the jar in the first place?

Hermes had been performing his duty of escorting the recently dead to their new home in the Underworld when he first had spotted Hades with the jar. There was a special case involving a young man who died at the very moment he committed his first intentional lie. Hermes didn't know where to take this half-innocent, half-guilty lad so he went looking for Hades to get advice. That's when he saw the God of the Underworld fawning over the jar in one of his more hidden chambers. Hermes couldn't believe his eyes.

When Pandora disappeared everyone thought she took the jar with her since neither had been seen in years. Hermes wondered how Hades got the jar, and why he hadn't alerted any of the other gods about its return. Knowing the whereabouts of Pandora's Jar wasn't the kind of thing to keep secret. The gods had spent decades secretly scouring the earth for it. Hades must have had some reason, some *selfish* reason, for hiding the jar and guarding it so vigilantly.

Hermes kept the matter of the jar to himself, with a few discrete exceptions. All hell would break loose if the others gods knew that Hades had it, especially Zeus. They were already so preoccupied with man's more immediate problems that adding the issue of the jar to their lists of things to do wasn't wise. Besides, Hermes believed that once the jar found its way to the Grace those other problems would lessen if not disappear altogether. He also believed that if the jar stayed with Hades, the consequences could be too dire for the world to survive.

Hermes didn't know what, but he knew Hades was up to something. Until he was sure what that something was, he had to be careful. Hermes couldn't let Hades or the other Olympians know he knew about the jar before he had the chance to do with it what should have been done long ago.

But, until now, it wasn't the right time, and there wasn't a right way, or the right one. Until now. No, Hades mustn't be allowed to keep the jar. The Grace must discover it.

Hermes opened his arms and offered his body up to the air as he flew to Athena's temple. He had an important message to deliver, and if he knew Hades and those dreadful Erinyes Sisters at all, he hadn't much time to deliver it. He flew on, faster.

CHAPTER 6
THE PROBLEM WITH PANDORA

CHARIS BARELY MADE IT to second period on time, no thanks to the ambush by Lauren and her entourage. The room was still buzzing with the chatter of students when Mr. Papadakis whistled the class to order. The distractions of dances, mean girls, and cute boys clouding Charis's thoughts cleared with the shrill whistle. It was a welcomed interruption. No matter how bad her day might be, English class always made it a little better. This was especially true when Mr. Papadakis, or "Mr. P" as the students called him, showed up as a substitute for Mrs. Nelson, who was out on maternity leave.

Mr. P was eager, exciting, and lacked the snide pessimism a lot of teachers had after their 7th or 8th year in the trenches. He loved teaching, and his enthusiasm made his students love what he taught, which for the past six weeks had been Greek mythology. He was the best teacher Charis had ever had and the thought of him leaving in a couple days after winter break bummed her out.

Since he'd taken over the class, Mr. P brought ancient Greece to life. The way he talked about the Greek gods, Charis would have sworn he knew them personally. He made them seem real, and like mythology was less myth and more magic; a magic that could be conjured at any moment and for any reason at all. Charis had begun seeing it that way too in her own life ... just like today during her confrontation with Lauren and her groupie friends. As Lauren snatched away her hope of going to the dance with Brady, Charis imagined the girl as one of those Harpy creatures Mr. P told them about. According to Greek mythology, Harpies eagerly went about their duty of snatching valuable things from people for the sole purpose of tormenting them.

If that isn't Lauren I don't know what is.

Charis chuckled to herself, imagining Lauren all birdlike with tattered feathers and gnarled claws.

"What's so funny?"

Charis looked up to see Brady standing above her. Her cheeks warmed at his presence. Now it was Brady she imagined as a middle school Greek Adonis, the God of Beauty.

"Well?" Brady continued with the half-smile that was Charis's weakness and Achilles Heel. Fearing she was making a fool of herself, Charis tried to pull her gaze from Brady's deep-brown eyes but couldn't. She mumbled "nothing" but it sounded more like "mothim" because her mouth was a desert. Charis rolled her eyes and wished for the ground to swallow her. She knew she'd eventually have to talk to her mom about this, whatever *this* was.

"Hmmm. You're strange, Charis Parks," he said, smiling. As Brady sat down next to her, Charis inhaled the smell of fabric softener wafting from his sweatshirt, which was the perfect shade of blue for his olive skin.

"Cool. If you won't tell me your secret, then we should get started. We've got a little more work to do on the end of the play — the moment of truth!"

The mention of "work" snapped Charis out of her Brady-inspired trance so she pulled out of her notebook, ready. Gabe and Emma joined them at the table too.

Mr. P had divided the class into groups, each contributing toward what would not only be a final grade for the semester, but also a play performed in front of the whole school Friday afternoon. One group worked on the set, creating ornate Corinthian columns and statues. Another created elaborate wardrobes made of long, flowing robes, decorative head garlands, and papier-mâchâ masks. Charis, Brady, Gabe, and Emma were all members of the small group selected to write the play for which all this building, sewing, and papier-mâchâing was necessary. For the past two weeks, the four of them had written and re-written the script to make sure it was perfect and ready for the performance. Before the end of each class, Mr. P checked their work to either give a thumbs up or suggest changes. With the play only days away, the group was pretty close to finished and only needed to polish the end. Mr. P said it wasn't dramatic enough.

The class assignment was to present its own version of one of the myths they'd studied together. Of all of the myths to choose from—the Twelve Labors of Hercules, Helen of Troy, and the Myth of King Midas, to name a few—the class selected Pandora's Jar as their final project.

The myth begins with Prometheus, the Titan who stole fire from Zeus, the Lightning God, and gave it to man. Zeus is outraged at the theft and vows revenge on the race of mankind because of it. Zeus orders Hephaestus, the God of Technology, to make a human woman—the first—out of clay. When the woman is created, Zeus then tells the other gods to give her gifts and talents like no other human in history. They do. The gods give her beauty, wisdom, wealth, and a host of other treasures. They decide to name her Pandora. It means "all-gifted one"' Zeus plots to give Pandora as a wife to Epimetheus, (brother of Prometheus, the Titan who stole the fire), but before he does, Zeus presents Pandora with one final gift—a jar.

Once Pandora is sent to Epimetheus, the girl's curiosity leads her to open Zeus's jar. According to the legend, her decision still plagues mankind this very day because within the jar was the worst imaginable evil. Zeus had placed malicious spirits of every sort inside his jar, and when Pandora opens it, she unleashes them upon the world where they still create pain and chaos even now.

Charis *loved* the story of Pandora's Jar and would have danced a happy dance when the class voted for it if she didn't care about embarrassing herself in front of Brady. For her, the story tried to answer the one question that bounced around in her head since she could remember: why? Why suffering? Why evil? Why were people capable of such meanness toward one another? It was also the story of beginnings: the beginning of women, marriage, choice, and consequences. And, it was downright scandalous, like those reality shows her mom was convinced would be the end of modern civilization. Charis couldn't explain it, but there was something about the story that intrigued her more than any other. But, it bothered her too.

She didn't understand how the gods could create Pandora as a punishment and not because they actually loved her. That hardly seemed fair. And Charis couldn't believe that they could just *give* Pandora away in marriage like she was property and not a human being. Didn't she have any say so? And it burned Charis up that of all of the gifts the gods gave to Pandora, it was the one she admired most, Pandora's curiosity, which led her to open the stupid jar. Curiosity was something Charis understood.

> ... *Aren't we supposed to be curious to learn?*
> ... *Didn't the gods know her curiosity would lead her to open the jar?*
> ... *If they did, isn't it their fault?*
> ... *Is it fair for the whole world to suffer because of what one woman did?*

Questions like these drove Charis crazy, and that's why she loved the story so much and begged her classmates to love it and vote for it too.

Together, the playwrights re-created the myth of Pandora's Jar in a play titled, *World of Woe: The Story of Pandora, a Jar, and the 5 o'clock News.* They called it WOW for short. While the four writers stayed true to the original myth, Mr. P encouraged them to add modern examples of the problems that remain since Pandora opened the jar. That part was easy. All they had to do was watch the news or go online to find that the legacy of Pandora's Jar was still alive and well. Whether in the arrest of some Hollywood starlet or in the world's wars that scared the daylights out of Charis, the jar's plague was everywhere.

On the evenings that Charis browsed the news online, she often daydreamed about meeting Pandora. The two were always dressed in beautiful, long gowns, and even though Charis could hardly picture herself all dolled up like that, she went with it. Charis imagined strolling along with Pandora in some garden on stony paths and stopping occasionally to admire a butterfly or climbing ivies or something like that. They'd talk about how little the gods understood humans and how much less humans understood the gods. And then, even though Charis would assure Pandora that she admired her curiosity, she'd do her best to warn her against following it. She imagined herself trying to convince Pandora to leave that awful jar closed. But even as she daydreamed, Charis knew that she couldn't have resisted opening the jar either.

Mr. P shuffled his way toward Charis's desk, dragging his left foot behind him. When he was born there was something wrong with one of his legs. He told the class about it on his first day just to get all of the staring and questions out of the way.

"Charis," he said once he reached her and the other writers. "I really enjoyed your essay comparing and contrasting Eve and Pandora. You had some interesting stuff in there. You and I should discuss it further."

Charis smiled before glancing nervously at her friends.

"Overachieving again, huh?" Gabe joked, elbowing her.

"Speaking of *achieving,* how are we coming?" Mr. P asked the writing group, raising his thick, black eyebrows.

"We're really close, Mr. P. We're going to nail it," Emma answered, excited and smiling. She was like that all the time. Emma had cheered for her brother's pop warner football team ever since she was three years old and *everything* that came out of her mouth sounded like a rousing cheer.

"*But,*" Brady interjected, "we are having a little bit of trouble." Although Brady wasn't a fan of Greek mythology (he thought the gods behaved like anything but) he was still really smart, and a good writer. Charis was glad he'd been chosen for the group ... for lots of reasons.

"We're stuck with Pandora at the jar, Mr. P. When she's just about to open it, what do you think she's thinking? She doesn't know the damage she's about to do, does she?"

"What makes you believe that, Brady?" Mr. P responded to *that* question like he did to *every* question, with another question.

"Well, I don't think she does," Gabe answered before Brady could. "I mean, how could she be trying to be evil if evil was still trapped inside the jar, right? Am I right?" He was pleased with his own cleverness. "I think she was just curious. I mean, she's got this gift from Zeus and of course she'd want to see what was inside it. I would."

There were nods of agreement.

"Okay," Mr. P said, "now that we've gotten clear on that, what do you think she does immediately afterwards, when all of the evil spirits have escaped the jar?"

Charis thought she saw her teacher's eyes soften. *With pity?*

"What do you do when you realize the whole world is different ... *worse* because of something you've done? Do you give up and think all is lost? Or, do you try to make it right again?"

"You try," everyone but Charis whispered. She was too busy biting her bottom lip trying to stop herself from asking the questions she felt coming.

"Why?" Charis finally blurted. She couldn't resist. "Why should she try to fix it? She wasn't really the one to mess things up, was she? The gods were."

There were audible groans around the table. None of the writers wanted to go through this again, the Q & A of Charis Parks. They were *never* going to get through with this script the way things were going.

"Aw, come on Charis," Emma said, still managing her constant smile despite her frustration. "We've been through this already. It's just the right thing to do. Of course she'd want to fix it. It doesn't matter whose fault it is."

"I know, but ..."

"Charis, come on," Gabe said, messing up his already messed up hair. "Nothing we say is going to change your mind anyway. So, can't we just agree that it's the right thing to do and not have to understand the why part of it? This time? Sometimes you just have to do the right thing because it's the right thing. Okay?"

He looked at her the same pleading way he looked at her every time they came to an impasse like this. Charis saw that Brady and Emma had the same expressions on their faces too. *Sigh.*

"Fine," Charis said. "It's the 'right' thing. Who cares *why!*"

Mr. P seemed entertained by the disagreement. It had only been a few weeks since he'd gotten to know Charis, but he'd already come to expect and maybe even appreciate this curious streak within her.

"Then go on and get to it," Mr. P said, clapping his meaty hands before limping away. "You can do it, that's why I chose you. After all, the fate of the world is at stake and ..." with his eyes trained on Charis he insisted, " ... it's in *your* hands."

Charis reached behind her to scratch her itching birthmark.

CHAPTER 7
FROM THE DARK OF NIGHT TO THE LIGHT OF DAY

The jar. They must get it. They cannot fail. It was of the utmost importance to Lord Hades, and so it was to them also.

"The time is now. Now is the time." Tisiphone grinned showing her jagged teeth. Her smile looked painful on her owl-like face. Deep within the endless caverns of the Underworld, the Erinyes Sisters stood hunched in a tight circle. Their black wings were lifted protectively around one another. As their heads nodded in agreement, the serpents dangling from them came alive with anticipation. Tisiphone looked directly into the blood-red eyes of her sister Alecto with her own.

"Alecto, the task falls to you. To you this task falls." The black serpents coiling around each of their faces hissed their dreadful affirmation. Hades chose Alecto to go to the earth this time because her face, though altogether ugly and severe, resembled a human's more readily than the others. The plan was for her to pose as an art curator, giving her much-needed access to the jar and the chance to take care of any loose ends if necessary.

"I am ready, Tisiphone," Alecto replied. Her small, pinched mouth moved, but it made no sound. In this realm of darkness where the Erinyes Sisters reign, most of the swirling sounds came from the suffering. Alecto had grown to enjoy the wails of the evil dead so much that she hated adding her own voice to their noise for fear it would take away from her pleasure. In the presence of her sisters, she spoke primarily by using her thoughts.

"Ready, am I," she mouthed. As if to prove it, Alecto fluttered her dagger-like wings high above her sisters and let out an audible and ancient shriek. The poor souls close by began to weep in agony, as though the knife of Alecto's scream cut right through them.

"Quiet!" shouted Tisiphone. She turned her head halfway around like an owl to glare behind her. The crying ceased.

"Quiet, you pitiful fools!" Fire spat from Tisiphone's mouth, a warning in flames.

"You will retrieve the jar and bring it back to Hades. To Hades, you must bring it. The jar," Tisiphone continued after turning her head back to her sisters.

"The jar remains where I have told you, Alecto. You will find it where I have said," Megaera murmured beneath her poorly disguised disappointment.

The formlessness of her shapeless and shadowed face could not even hide her shame. She was the one who had failed to bring it back at the first attempt. It was her fault, her blame. The torment she loved to inflict on others now caused her own head to hang low in disgrace.

"You will find it!"

The word "you" floated gray from Megaera's lips and pointed a skinny finger at Alecto.

"I will find it, Megaera," assured Alecto, mutely. She breathed in her sister's word "you" and inwardly vowed to win back Megaera's honor. "Find it I will and bring it back to our Lord Hadesss, thisss jar."

"You must use caution, Alecto," Megaera warned. "Caution, you must use. Much has changed since last we walked freely among the humans."

The sisters were silent for a moment. They understood the danger. The humans had advanced in a great many ways. They knew more and feared less. The terror that used to keep man from venturing too close to the shadows between himself and the gods was waning. The Erinyes Sisters could hardly rely on subtle fear to ensure their conceal-ment anymore. The bumps in the night, sudden cold chills, or strange, unexplained coincidences that once made humans run away now sent them running *toward* potential dangers ... with recording devices... just in case.

Should Alecto be discovered, there was no punishment great enough for the sisters to suffer. While they were accustomed to giving punishment, they were not ready to receive it. Megaera was proof of that. After she failed at the museum, she dug herself a grave and had to be dragged out of it by her sisters after her meeting with Hades. Only the wet aloneness of her burial made her feel any better. Still, the task must be completed. The risk must be taken.

"It must be returned," Megaera started. The words darted from her mouth and into the thick, hot air in red.

"It must be returned," Tisiphone repeated.

"It mussst be returned," Alecto shouted using her voice.

"It must be returned!"

The sisters raged within their eternal circle until they and the souls around them were in a frenzied uproar. When their cries reached their peak, Alecto spread the horrible wings that would carry her from the dark of her home to the dark she would bring upon the earth with her.

"It mussst be returned!"

CHAPTER 8
NIKE NEARLY BLOWS IT

"Aren't you a little old to be playing with dolls, Sunny?" Presley ruffled Charis's curly mane with his large football-playing hands. She sat absent-mindedly at the kitchen table, rolling her splendid little keychain in her hands while her dad finished dinner. With so much going on at school, Charis forgot to ask Gabe about the charm that found its way in her backpack.

"What is that anyway?" her brother asked.

"I don't know … some kind of figurine. It was in my backpack. I think Gabe put it there," Charis said. She held it up to Presley's face, which for the moment appeared settled somewhere between boy and man.

"It's pretty, huh?"

Presley raised his eyebrows.

"Sure?" Presley replied.

"Hey, how was your driving lesson this morning? You ready to be my chauffer?"

Presley laughed her joke away and grabbed the plates to set the table.

"Do we need a fifth?"

"No. Gabe is at his mom's tonight. Speaking of moms, where's ours?"

Charis placed her keychain on the table to help Presley with the silverware.

"She had to work late tonight," her dad said as he spooned out cheesy pasta onto a serving plate. "Something came up with that Getty exhibition, but she should be here any minute." On cue, the garage door closed as Charis's mom entered the house.

"Hey guys," she sighed. She threw her coat, purse, tote bag, and everything else that weighed her down onto the counter and gave Evan a hug that looked more like a lean. It had been that kind of day.

"Smells good, babe," she said.

"Well, your timing is impeccable. Dinner is served," Evan boasted.

Around the table, Evan blessed the food.

"Where's Gabe?" Mona asked.

"With his mom," Charis answered.

"That's good, right?"

Charis shrugged her shoulders. "I don't know. I guess it could be."

"Well, we can certainly hope so, honey. Pres, how was the driving lesson?" Mona posed the question gently, not wanting to bring up any dreadful memories of their failed attempts together.

"It was fine, Mom," Presley responded. He smirked. "Mr. Hall is actually a *good* driving teacher."

Mona cut her eyes at his attempt at humor. "Don't be a snark, dude. Charis, what about your test?"

"I think I did good. I think. But, that's not even the best part of the day," she said thinking about the finishing touches they'd made on the play in English. "Or the worst," she said, remembering Lauren, her Harpy friends, and the dance with Brady that wasn't. Before she could even explain any of it her mother interrupted.

"Well, my day wasn't the greatest at all," Mona sighed, pouring a glass of wine.

"Here it is Monday and I'm in the middle of getting all of the last-minute details together for the museum Friday night when Richard from the Getty calls. When we first got the account, he was the fellow who was so hard to please. Remember? He must have rejected five or six pitches before we came up with a concept he liked. To his credit, he was absolutely right because the campaign has been amazing. Perfect, really. The billboards. The posters. The online ads. Everything. Perfect. But today, he's on the phone in a panic telling me how they might have to postpone or cancel the exhibition altogether!"

Charis's heart sank. Going to the museum made up for not going to the dance, even not going to the dance with Brady. She put her fork full of asparagus down. Her appetite was gone just like her Friday night at the Getty.

"Apparently, the curator in charge of the exhibition disappeared without a trace. Gone. Richard didn't think they could find anyone else to manage it on such short notice. Can you believe that? After all that hard work? I was hot! I mean ... *hot!*"

"Sorry, babe," Evan said, trying to comfort her.

"I know, right? But, long story short, everything is okay now. After worrying about it all day, Richard called back just as I was leaving to say they found someone. His name is Al Ecto, and he's from Greece. He's supposed to be the world's foremost expert on Greek antiquities. It looks like after having my stomach in knots all day, we're good to go!" Mona smiled directly at her daughter.

From the moment Mona told Charis about winning the Getty account, the girl couldn't contain her excitement. She went on and on to her mom about her substitute teacher Mr. P, Greek mythology, and Pandora. Mona was crushed at the thought of disappointing her baby.

"I'm so relieved," Mona said, exhaling a deep breath.

Charis released the breath she hadn't realized she'd been holding too.

Thank God!

"I thought that I'd offer Mr. Al Ecto a personal thank you on behalf of the firm and host a dinner for him here. Nothing fancy, just us, a few people from the office who worked on the account, and a handful from the Getty," Mona said. "He arrives tomorrow, so I'm thinking dinner on Wednesday evening. Can we all be here?"

"Sure. That'll be great," Evan said. "I'm really glad it all worked out ... for poor Richard's sake. He'd rather deal with a missing curator than a disappointed Mona, trust me," Evan laughed.

"Whatever, and yay!" Mona squealed. "I'll have it catered so that it won't be too much trouble. Too bad Mr. Ecto missed out on this though," she said taking another bite of her pasta.

Evan raised his glass. "A toast to your mom, her firm, the Getty, the gods, and Mr. Al Ecto!" The family all touched glasses amidst their cheers.

"Hear, hear!" Charis chimed in. She raised her glass of water to take a drink and what she saw through its bottom could only be described as impossible. The new keychain standing next to her plate *moved*. It was subtle, and on the face—a small change in expression. For a split second, the keychain, once serene and lovely, looked grim and worried. It was a weird look for any doll to have. Charis slammed her glass down on the table, rattling everyone's plates.

"What tha? No way!" She picked up the figurine and gawked at it in her clutched hands.

"Something wrong, Sunny?" Evan asked.

Charis looked up to see her family staring at her like she was crazy.

Maybe I am …

She shook her head side to side. "No. Nothing," she stammered. "I just … I just thought. I mean. I thought …"

I thought, what?

"Oh, never mind," she mumbled.

CHAPTER 9
VICTORY FLIES AWAY

THEY HAD ENJOYED a long time of celestial peace. Nike hadn't been called to the battlefield in years. Not since the Titan War, and that was waged a lifetime ago. It wasn't as if there hadn't been skirmishes within the heavens on occasion; gods can be so easily offended and coaxed into combat over the silliest things.

Such egos, she smirked.

Nor had the realm of Gaia, the earth, been free of bloodshed. The earth's soil runs red with it too often, and for too many frivolous reasons. Land disputes, possession of resources, political gain, temple rituals.

As if any of it belongs to them anyway. You would think they'd learn … but Nike knew better.

She, above all, understood that both men and gods were foolish in matters of war: eager to declare, slow to concede. Still, she was greatly surprised when Hermes came to her and Athena that day in Athena's temple. The look of urgency on his face was unsettling, even for a warrior like herself.

"So," Athena said breathlessly, "The prophecy is true. The jar has been found. The time is now." Her lovely face could not hide her concern. She looked as if she'd seen the head of Medusa snarling from within Hermes's words.

"Of course it is, sister." Hermes chided, his words an ocean of trouble. "Did you doubt it?"

"No … No, but surely I hadn't anticipated a possible problem with Hades," she responded.

Athena was almost always a portrait of restraint and control. While not particularly known for her beauty, she was beautiful. However, outward beauty wasn't something Athena necessarily valued. What Athena most treasured was her wisdom, her intuition, and her acumen for war. This present moment of frustration disoriented her, and it showed in her furrowed brow.

"I need some time to think, to devise a plan, I …"

"We haven't any time, Athena!" Hermes raised his voice with red and combustible energy. The atmosphere began to change into something threatening. The Messenger God quickly turned away. He needed to control his temper. The last thing he wanted to do was provoke Athena. She was kind, but cunning as well. He … *they* needed all of her energies focused on the problem at hand and not on how to outwit Hermes in a verbal sparring.

He continued, this time calm and cool like the breeze now circling them.

"We haven't any *more* time, noble Athena … I mean, beyond the thousands of years we've had already."

Hermes looked into Athena's gray eyes and summoned the strength he realized they both needed. Athena nodded, understanding. In that twinkling, she returned back to her rational and temperate self, greatly resembling the marble statues sculpted by devotees in her honor. Calm. Stoic. Steady. Wise. She turned her gaze to Nike who stood guard at the temple doors.

"Come here, Warrior Sister," Athena said.

Nike knelt at Athena's feet and bowed her head. As Athena said a prayer of wisdom over her, the words pouring out like water, Nike could all but see her journey ahead. She was built for this moment, and every other embattled one. She epitomized strength, speed, and courage. Nike was, in every respect, the Goddess of Victory.

"My dear, Nike," Athena said looking down at her, "you are prepared."

Nike held Athena's gray eyes with her own emerald ones—the moment so green and fertile with possibility and promise. For centuries, she and Athena had imagined this day and strategized every possible offense. Those strategies changed with every era of man, from the Dark Ages when men thought the world was flat, to now, the age of the iPad, when men thought the round world fit on a flat surface. That today was *the* day, and that this time was *the* time, was almost more than she could take … she'd dreamed about it for so long.

Nike's heart raced inside her chest. Her once green eyes flashed red and the warrior in her awakened. If the eyes are the windows to the soul, then Nike's were magnifying glasses. The excitement pulsing through her body caused her iridescent wings to tremble with the anticipation of flight. There were no more words needed. Nike was electric and alive, set on fire by the memory of every battle she'd ever fought. Her fiery energy reached out into Athena's temple, setting it ablaze in vibrations of reds, oranges, yellows, and pinks. This task, this mission, would be the story of legend.

The growing fervor between Nike and Athena drew Hermes close to the goddesses. The thrill of the inevitable struggle for the destiny of their worlds was irresistible to the competitor within him.

"Go to the Fates. Make our offering to the sacred sisters and they will assist you as they have sworn they would." Athena spoke unemotionally and with dead calm against Nike's electric charge in the air.

"Go, sure goddess!" Athena continued. "Go, and tell no one!"

Athena need not have issued that warning. They all understood what would happen should the others find out. If Zeus, Athena's father and King, heard even a whisper about Hades and the jar, the war of the Titans would be a mere bedtime story compared to what would happen. Zeus could not know. They had to contain this. No one must know but them.

"As sure as my name is Victory, I shall not fail," Nike proclaimed. Her eyes now glowed a cool blue like the ice running cold through her veins. She stood and turned her attention west, the direction of the Fates.

"By Zeus, I shall not."

The three gods embraced and Hermes blessed Nike with a prayer of luck. It had begun, as they were told one day it would.

"By Zeus," vowed Hermes.

"By Zeus," swore Athena.

Without a word more, Nike bounded from Athena's temple into the open, cloudless sky. Her massive, radiating wings tore through the air of Olympus. To the Fates, those sovereign sisters, she'd go.

Nike sped. As time and space melted around her, nothing more than wind running its fingers through her ebony hair, a grin slowly grew across her golden face. She knew the journey ahead would be fraught with mortal danger and reveled at the idea of battle.

What good is it to be the Goddess of Victory with no war to fight and win?

Nike pierced through the darkening sky.

CHAPTER 10
TEMPTING FATE

THEY WERE WAITING FOR HER when she arrived.

But of course.

Perched on a crag near their remote cave, the three Fates watched for Nike with their beguiling faces lifted toward the starry sky. Upon stools of gray and black-flecked stone, the women sat close to one another in a semi-circle, their hands busy with the constant spinning, measuring, and cutting that was their duty. Though their faces were perfectly still, gazing heavenward toward the descending Nike, their hands moved with such speed they appeared nothing but a blur; Klotho twisting her white thread, Lakhesis measuring the thread with her orange rod, and finally Atropos snipping the thread with her sharp, greedy shears.

Klotho, birth. Lakhesis, life. Atropos, death.

The threads, each symbolizing the life of a god, man, woman, child, animal, or any living thing, gathered unceremoniously around the feet of the three sisters until some unnamed wind carried them away to wherever it pleased.

Though Nike's bravery was legendary even among the gods, Athena instructed her to be humble in the presence of the Fates, not courageous. Nike agreed. She set aside the battle cry that constantly sounded within her heart and assumed, instead, a perfect peace. After all, there was no challenge the Fates could not win with a simple snip of a thread from Atropos's deadly scissors. Nike knew the sisters held her thread in their hands as well. It was better to be humble before such power than courageous. Courage is too easily mistaken for pride, and everyone knows that pride goes before a fall.

Before placing her sandaled foot to the ground, Nike bowed her head. Her black hair fell like sheets around her face. The Warrior Goddess extended an open palm before the Fates. In it lay a slender, purple vial. Its contents were alive with colorful, liquid motion. Nike raised her equally purple eyes to the sisters, hoping they were pleased with what they saw. The baby-faced Klotho smiled at her, revealing a toothless, wet grin.

"You may come to us, girl," she said, the words spitty in her mouth and sounding like a baby's babble.

"Oou mah kuh to ussh gurh."

Though ancient, Klotho had the appearance of a newborn babe: her cheeks, rosy and plump; her eyes, sparkling in newness; her hair, nothing more than tufts of blonde wisps upon her round head. It made sense. She was the one who spun the thread from which all life came, from which all creatures drew their first, fresh breaths.

Nike set herself down upon the jagged earth gently, reverently, her wings tucked in close behind her. She was careful not to step on any of the fallen threads. Regardless of how casually the sisters wove, measured, and cut their thread, it felt like holy ground to Nike. She considered the threads racing in and out of the sisters's hands and wondered about the lives they represented. How many dreams were fulfilled and how many cut short? How many destinies reached and how many never realized? Another gust of wind gathered the threads and whisked them away into the night air.

"Bring it closer, Warrior Goddess," Lachesis, the middle sister, invited. Her hands never ceased to measure out how much life one soul might have over another, or what kind of life it might be. She was the keeper of destinies, of experience, of opportunity, and purpose. Lachesis was lovely. Her almond-shaped eyes were kind; her petal pink lips, soft and prone to smiling; her chestnut hair, shiny and free. Her face glowed with health and vitality. Her eyes shone with the pure essence of life in its prime, when it was well lived, appreciated, and seized.

Nike stepped forward, lifting the crystal container with her fingers where Lachesis might study it. It looked beautiful in the light of Artemis's moon. Raising her soft eyes from the vial, Lachesis looked up at Nike and gave her a warm smile.

"You have honored us with this offering," Lachesis assured, her voice peaceful and calm. "It is acceptable."

Nike bowed her head again, this time to hide the relief on her face. It had been a difficult offering to conceive. What does one give to the Fates in exchange for their help? The sisters already possess within their busy hands the most valuable thing to any god or man: life and death. It was Athena who thought up a suitable gift, her wisdom more than just myth and legend. It was true that the sisters controlled the destinies of gods and men alike. It was also true that such power inspired more fear of the Fates than love for them. The sisters knew this, and had never been able to live happily among the other gods because of it. They exiled themselves to the outskirts of Olympus, keeping company only with each other and their threads.

It was unfortunate, and they did not understand it completely. Fashioned by Fate themselves, it was their duty in life to determine the lives of others. They were merely doing what they were created to do. Their inability to understand how their incessant spinning, measuring, and cutting upset those whose threads they spun, measured, and cut left them agitated; not the best mood given their responsibilities.

Athena reasoned that what the Fates didn't have in empathy, she could give them through wisdom. In exchange for their help in retrieving the jar, she would give them something equally valuable. She would give the Fates insight into the true nature of all their spinning, measuring, and cutting. She would give them an understanding beyond their simple routine, which was driven by nothing more than duty.

In the privacy of her own temple, Athena sat in meditation for days thinking about the mysteries and blessings of life. She contemplated the celebration of birth and the mourning in death. She mulled over causes and cures, peace and war, plenty and lack. When at last her reflections caused her to weep the bittersweet tears of life's joys and sorrows, Athena bottled her tears in the little purple vial that Nike now held before the Fates. An offering. An elixir. A liquid enlightenment into the mysteries of life.

"Ladies," Nike said. "I've been asked to humbly remind you of the cost of this sacrifice, both to its giver and to you, its recipients, should you partake."

At this, Atropos, the eldest sister, spoke from dust and age. "We needn't be reminded." She looked into Nike's golden eyes with her milky ones, all the while opening and closing, opening and closing, opening and closing her shears.

"We know the risks, valiant goddess."

The deep folds of her face closed in on one another and formed themselves into a wrinkled smile. She, like Klotho, had no teeth. She, like Klotho, had no hair. The few strands of silver she had waved at nothing on top of her head.

"My sisters and I will weigh the consequences among us," she wheezed.

The hesitation was appropriate. Since the beginning, the Fates determined which souls would be born, what kinds of lives they would live, and for how many days. They did this out of duty, out of destiny, and without emotion. However, should they drink from Athena's tears and become awakened to the very heart of life, would they remain committed in their duties? Could they still spin, measure, and cut as was their purpose? Or, with their eyes now opened, would they be unable, and alter the histories of gods and men in some unknown and tragic way?

These were the questions.

"Drinking Athena's potion is not the only risk we are taking here, is it?" Atropos rasped. The smile that struggled on her face finally gave way to a more comfortable grimace.

The Fates had scoffed when Hermes first flew to them from the Underworld with his pleadings and plans. They were completely unimpressed with his voice so full of earthquake and rumbling. But he persisted, speaking words of truth. He left the sisters no option but to consider his concern and ultimately involve themselves in its relief.

The Messenger God told the Fates about Hades hoarding the jar. He expressed his fear that, should the jar remain in Hades's possession, catastrophe would result. At first, the Fates hardly listened to Hermes. Why should they intervene with destiny? They did not judge it 'good' or 'bad'. It just was. But, when he told them that she who they foretold had arrived upon the earth, the sisters listened with rapt attention.

"How do you know?" Klotho asked him.

"We've suspected the time was near for years." Hermes had answered with a sigh the sound of a waterfall. "When the constellation Libra tipped its scales, we knew the time had come. It took a while to locate her. Navigating the earth undetected has become a Herculean task; modern man's technology is to blame, of course. But when the stars guided our search to North America, we finally found her in California."

"Tell us about her," Lakhesis pleaded. Her face glowed with exuberance.

"What I gather from the demigod we've assigned to her, she's thirteen years of age, smart, kind, and ... curious," he answered with a lightness and sun.

Atropos croaked from her sunken lips. "And you are sure it is her? She bears the Mark?"

"The demigod, Erichthonius, has confirmed it. As I've explained, the child lives in California where there are beaches she loves. He saw the Mark on her back while she swam in the surf." His voice turned to stone, "She is here, just as *you* prophesied at the beginning. The Grace has arrived to release hope into the world."

For the first time in the *history* of time, the Fates stopped spinning, measuring, and cutting with their hands. Birth, life, and death stood still.

"You can see why it is important that we free the jar from Hades's hands and help it into hers."

The Fates resumed their duties.

"Hades interferes with fate for reasons unknown to us," Lakhesis said to her sisters. "It is not our custom to meddle in such affairs, but I don't see how we can refrain with so much at stake. Admittedly, sisters, we know not what motivates Hades, but the truth remains that the jar is not his. If he is acting as an obstacle to the Grace finding it, then we must do our duty to restore fate's original path ... a path that leads it directly to her. We must give her the opportunity to live her destiny."

Klotho squealed like a happy baby. "We will help you, Hermes," she giggled.

The agreements they made that day led to Nike standing before them now wondering if they had changed their minds.

"Set the vial down, goddess, and kneel," gurgled the baby-faced Klotho. Nike sank to her knees and laid Athena's vial beside her. It tinkled as it touched the slate ground.

"I see you question our commitment," the aged Atropos breathed heavily. "You question if we will be faithful to our word or if we have changed our minds instead." She grew weary. The effort to speak was difficult and meant for younger, newer strength.

Nike lowered her black eyes in shame.

"We understand the risk we are taking," Atropos slowly continued. "It is for you we have concern." Kindness emerged from beneath her wrinkles as she smiled at Nike again.

"Dear Nike," Lakhesis said. "Are you sure of *your* decision? There is no guarantee against failure. And, unless the Grace succeeds, what we do here today cannot be undone." Nike lifted her blazing ruby eyes to the sisters.

"I am sure!" she huffed, sounding dangerously close to courageous.

"So be it."

From her golden spool, Klotho began weaving a new thread for a new Nike. Her fingers darted in and out of the chord. As it stretched longer and longer, Nike shrank shorter and shorter in a welter of twisting and turning. Nike spun and writhed in mid-air, gritting her teeth against the pain that transformed and miniaturized her. At last, the sister knitted her final knot and Nike exploded, an eruption of extreme light and colors.

When the smoke cleared, there Nike stood, a mere fraction of her former and statuesque self. She looked up high at the Fates who looked down low at her. Their hands had resumed their typical obligations, and the dropping threads crashed like logs around the little Nike.

"Go, wee goddess," crowed Atropos, her voice booming in Nike's tiny little ears. "Take flight with your wee wings ... shoo! Shoo! Go, help the girl. That is your destiny."

Nike bowed in gratitude before buzzing off into the navy night sky. It would take a long time and an enormous effort to reach

Charis, the Grace, but Nike eventually made it. When she did, she fluttered in exhaustion to the bottom of the girl's backpack and waited there to be discovered.

* * *

After Charis's outburst at dinner, the girl abruptly excused herself from the table, quickly cleaned the kitchen (it was her night) and ran upstairs to her bedroom, skipping a few steps along the way.

For the next hour or more, Charis held Nike in her hands, examining her at every angle. She placed Nike's crystal body beneath the lamp on her dresser causing her to refract in all manner of vibrant colors. Streams of reds, blues, yellows, greens, purples, and oranges splashed the walls of Charis's bedroom every time she turned the little goddess in her hands. She studied Nike's face in the bright light, twisting her this way and that, trying to determine if what had happened at the dinner table was even possible. Nike maintained a fixed face under the scrutiny. The time to reveal everything to Charis was coming; during dinner with her family was not it.

Nike couldn't believe she had nearly blown her cover. Then again, she couldn't believe the audacity of the Erinyes Sisters either.

Mr. "Al Ecto" ... by Zeus!

When the child was asleep, Nike would have to tell Athena and Hermes about Alecto's plan to pose as a curator for the Getty Museum. They needed to act quickly if they were going to stay ahead of Hades. Charis had to be informed, soon. Otherwise, they would be too late because Hades was already making his move. It was ridiculous, but clearly they'd underestimated Hades, his greed for the jar, and the lengths to which he was willing to go to get it back. At dinner, Nike's shock landed briefly on her face, presently the sole object of Charis's fascination.

Charis finally set Nike down to do her homework. Nike watched Charis breeze through math and chew her fingernails over biology. After she finished her homework, Charis Skyped with Andy. She didn't mention her suspicions about Nike, and Nike hoped it meant they were waning. Instead, the two friends talked about the latest episode of *Glee*, the sloppy way Mrs. Milner always applied her red lipstick, and the Greek mythology project they had only days to finish and perform. At the mention of the names of her fellow gods, Nike allowed herself to glow a pale pink. Later on, Charis and Gabe texted one another, but again, the girl wrote nothing about the dinner incident. Nike felt safe that Charis had rationalized it away.

At the end of the evening, Charis put on her pajamas and kissed her family goodnight before hopping into her bed.

"Whoops!" she said, jumping up and running across the carpeted floor to the dresser where Nike stood frozen. "I forgot about you."

She placed the goddess on the nightstand next to her bed. Charis laid back down, her hair a tangled nest around her. She stared at Nike with her wide brown eyes just as she had the night before.

"Well, good night little angel or whatever you are. I'm watching you, and if I didn't know better, I'd think you're watching me too." Charis yawned before shutting off the light. In the dark, Nike permitted herself a smile.

TUESDAY

All is change; all yields its place and goes.

—EURIPIDES

CHAPTER 11
LIKE AN EDEN

CHARIS WAS IN THE PALACE again. The familiar golden light shined all around her. Her feet lifted from the ground and she began her nightly glide.

As Charis floated down the hall, she noticed something different about tonight. The pictures she'd come to know so well were all gone. In their place hung mirrors. Lots of them. Charis watched her reflection come in and out of the surfaces as she slowly drifted by. Her ringlets rose like waves behind her as she floated toward the largest one and hovered there.

Maybe it was the gold light shining everywhere, maybe it was the fanciness of the place—whatever it was, Charis thought she looked different. Maybe even special. The thought caught her by surprise. She would never think she was better than anyone else. Her grandma used to say, "We all God's chillin', baby" in the Georgia drawl that reminded Charis of peach pie and sweet tea. Charis believed her too. But tonight, admiring her own reflection, Charis felt something ... *heard* something ... that whispered *special*.

When Charis turned four years old, she and her mom drove the scenic route up California's coast to Camarillo every June for fresh strawberries. For hours they handpicked red, ripe, shiny strawberries, fussing over every one like it was the last. At some point, beneath the shine of California's best sun, Mona and Charis would exchange a look only they knew. Glancing side to side, they'd carefully sift through their baskets of berries, pluck out the very best, sweetest, reddest one, and when they were sure no one was looking, they'd eat it. Charis would laugh as the juice ran down her mother's chin.

The hours the two spent driving, windows down, to the farm were special. The way Mona hummed as she knelt next to her daughter in the fields was special. The smell of sugar, the buzz of bees, and the feel of the thick, fuzzy strawberry leaves were special. The secret of the sweet, stolen berry enjoyed beneath wide-brimmed hats was special.

That's how Charis felt now looking at herself in the mirror. She felt strawberry-special, like the one spotted in the basket among many and chosen as a secret between mother and daughter as the sweetest thing.

As Charis stood there smiling at herself, the mirror slowly fogged over as a soft mist came from behind and warmed the back of her neck.

"What tha?" she whispered.

Charis closed her eyes. After giving it much thought, she wrote the word 'special' on the foggy mirror. To her immediate wonder, "special" faded and disappeared beneath a fresh fog. In its place the word "chosen" appeared, written by invisible hands. Charis quickly turned around but saw no one behind her. A seed of panic started to grow within her chest.

Charis moved away from the mirrors and flew farther down the long hall. It narrowed and led to a single door. She pushed the big, bronze door and found that it opened into a beautiful, plush garden that looked like a postcard. There were hanging vines with yellow and orange blooms, birds singing their best songs from lush trees, and deer quietly lapping water from a meandering stream. It was unreal.

Charis stood at the doorway in awe as she peered through the thick green leaves. Even as she wondered if she should go in, she knew that she would. She also knew that once she went through that door there would be no going back, wherever "back" was. Charis took a deep breath and flew inside.

"Oh, good! I was told you were a curious child." At the sound of the voice, overwhelming joy and fear balled themselves together in the pit of Charis's stomach.

"I … I" stuttered Charis.

I am dreaming, she reminded herself.

"I am relieved to see that it's true," the voice continued. There was a concentration of light just beyond the draping vines. When Charis parted them, she saw a radiant woman standing there, waiting for her.

"Well … come in, Charis. I've anticipated this moment when I could finally meet you."

Charis floated through the greenery toward the sun-kissed woman shining in the middle of the garden. She was, by far, its most lovely and exotic thing. Her pale purple robe hugged her tall body effortlessly and gathered at her waist with a golden rope. Purple and red flowers decorated her short blonde hair that shined like diamonds.

"Who … who are you?"

"Oh, do forgive me," the woman said. "My name is Athena."

The goddess paused, looking for any show of recognition. Charis drew her breath in and cupped her hands to her mouth before her words came rushing out.

"Athena! Also referred to as Pallas Athena. The goddess of wisdom, courage, inspiration, civilization, law and justice, mathematics, strength, strategy, the arts, crafts, and skill, and you just name it really." Charis gasped another long breath and continued.

"Athena was born to Zeus and Metis. After Zeus made it with Metis, he swallowed her. Bizarre I know, but he was afraid she would have his children and they would be more powerful than he was. What he didn't know was that Metis was already pregnant! See, later on Zeus had this awful headache. It was so bad that his head split wide open! And, when that happened, Athena … I mean, *you* popped out, fully grown and dressed for battle!" It was Charis's best wiki recital ever.

Athena laughed—the sound of pure joy. When she finally composed herself, she gazed at Charis. The girl found the goddess's eyes alarming, piercing right down to the soul. But they were also warm and inviting. "It looks like you're familiar with me."

"Oh, yes!" Charis answered, not thinking it was at all unusual to be engaged in a conversation with a figure from Greek mythology. All Charis noticed was how peaceful she felt, how calm. In the presence of the Goddess of Wisdom, it seemed the "whys" within Charis were quieted.

"Mr. P, I mean Mr. Papadakis, taught us all about you! He told us about your brothers and sisters, your enemies, your battles. Fascinating stuff."

"Well, I'm glad you've found it all so interesting." Athena reached out for Charis's hand and cupped it between her own. At her touch, Charis's eyes opened, as if for the first time. Wider. More. Clearer. And, not just to things like colors beyond colors or the iridescent, luminous, fine designs on the dragonflies buzzing about on wings that looked like stained glass, but invisible, secret, timeless things. Things thirteen-year-old girls either absolutely should or definitely should not know. Charis saw into the depths of people, ideas, and truth in the way that poets have forever struggled to describe. Something between a sigh and a cry escaped Charis's lips.

Athena released the girl's hand and, with it, her new insight also.

"What tha ... What was that?" Charis laughed rather nervously, opening and closing her hand.

Athena chuckled too. "Hmm, I can best describe it as something you'll never get used to but want to experience all the time." Athena placed a delicate finger to the center of Charis's forehead. "An awakening," she said.

"An awakening, " Charis repeated slowly.

"Charis, Mr. Papadakis has told me about you too." The words hung in the air and landed with a thud in Charis's mind. It was a shock much too real for a dream.

"What do you mean? How do you know Mr. P? Or me for that matter? I don't understand, what ...?

"*Ssshhh*. Hush now. All will be revealed. Come with me." Athena motioned her to a bench.

"Charis." Athena said her name like a song. "Such a beautiful name. You know in *my* language it means 'grace'."

"Yeah, I know!" Charis exclaimed. "When my brother was born something went wrong during his delivery. The doctors told my mom she wouldn't be able to have any more kids after that. My parents were devastated. That's the word my mom uses when she tells the story, 'devastated.' My dad said even though they knew it was a long shot, they kept hoping for a miracle, praying for one. Then, surprise, I came along when they weren't even trying. That's why they named me Charis. They said I was a 'child of grace'."

Charis frowned a little after she spoke. It was as if she just now realized what a tremendous burden being a "child of grace" might be.

"I like it," Athena said, recapturing Charis's attention. "Sometimes we face such terrible disappointments in our lives, don't we? Painful heartaches, gruesome wars, awful diseases ... it's all so worrying and unfortunate. It seems the presence of grace is the only way we can overcome our challenges and maintain our hope. Grace. Amazing grace." Silence settled in, at home in their conversation.

"Charis," Athena said, after taking a deep breath. "I'm about to tell you things you might have a hard time understanding, all right?"

"Okay," Charis said, shrugging her shoulders. It wasn't like she understood anything about these dreams so far anyway.

"I'm talking about things that not many people know or believe in anymore, but that are true nonetheless. Follow me."

Athena led Charis to the stream that ran in the center of the garden. As the two sat down in the cool, plush grass at its edge, the waters stopped flowing and became a smooth sheet of crystal-clear glass.

"I know your 'Mr. P' has told you about the story of Pandora, the first woman, crafted meticulously by the gods out of clay at Zeus's command. She was beautiful, nearly beyond measure, and endowed with every desirable attribute. Each god contributed to her making in his or her own unique way. We lavished upon her irresistible qualities and talents, indulging her with skill, intellect, and ambitions. She was a perfect first woman."

As Athena recounted Pandora's beginnings, scenes of her creation played upon the still water just like a movie. Charis saw, in vivid detail, the words Athena spoke come to life.

Upon the stream's surface was a lovely woman, whose shape and form emerged from the clay within the hands of her maker, Hephaestus, the God of Artisans. He fashioned her robust and shapely. He built her strong enough to be the mother of generations to come. Hephaestus smiled proudly at his creation. Then Charis saw the other gods' pilgrimage to Pandora, each bringing something to offer. A goddess, who Charis thought was Aphrodite because of her outrageously good looks, brought Pandora grace and beauty. A man with winged feet, who Charis guessed was Hermes, gave her the power of eloquent speech. A group of women, who Charis believed were the Graces, adorned her neck, hands, and wrists with dazzling jewels of every kind. Athena was there too, teaching Pandora needlework and weaving and dressing her in a fine silver gown and golden crown. The gods stood back and looked at their handiwork with pleasure.

"We loved Pandora, and took great pride in our finished work," Athena continued. "But the joy we felt was short-lived." The crystal waters turned dark and murky and churned with the black soot and sediment beneath them.

"We did not know that Zeus had commanded Pandora's creation as punishment for an offense committed against him by Prometheus, the Titan trickster who stole fire from Mt. Olympus and gave it to man."

Charis peered into the stormy waters nervously as a burly Prometheus ran down the mountain of Olympus carrying a burning ember above his head.

"We all know that he met with Zeus's punishment swiftly. To this day, Prometheus lays chained, helpless, to a rock, ever-tortured by the great eagle who eats his liver all day and repeats the gruesome duty with every new sunrise."

Charis turned her eyes away from the bloody scene of Prometheus wailing, chained and alive, with the eagle hungrily consuming his flesh. She looked at Athena instead, but her face was as gloomy as the stream.

"Prometheus's punishment may have been fitting, but the retribution Zeus took on mankind was …"

Athena stopped short of her near rebuke of the King of the Gods and decided on a wiser approach. She swirled the waters with her hands and the stream became crystal clear once again.

"When Zeus presented Pandora as a bride to Prometheus's brother Epimetheus, he received her gladly. Epimetheus had no reason to question Zeus's motives. After all, Pandora was everything a husband could want. She even came to him bearing her infamous jar, which they thought was an additional present from Zeus himself."

Charis saw Pandora, in all of her decorated splendor, bow before Epimetheus and show him the jar given her by Zeus.

"Their innocence of Zeus and his nefarious plot proved the death of the innocence of man, for within the jar was every imaginable evil.

Poverty, disease, aging, jealousy, greed, selfishness, war, fear, lies, murder, famine, death ..."

Horrible images of the worst creatures Charis had ever imagined flashed across the waters. There were red devils with rolling eyes in warped heads; misshapen troll-like creatures with their hungry mouths gaping open; and half-men, half-monsters with terrible, blank, zombie faces rotting away in decay. Silent tears flowed from Charis's eyes and Athena gathered her into her arms. For all of her wisdom, Athena forgot how emotional humans could be, how they often resisted the way things were and struggled beneath the hope that things could be different. Hope. Humans loved hope, however slight it might be. They needed it to survive.

"I'm sorry, sweet Charis. Truly, I am."

Athena's hands stirred the waters once more, causing the monstrous images to go away. She took her cool, wet hand and wiped away Charis's tears and then placed the girl's head against her chest. The two sat in momentary silence for a while.

"Because our Pandora was so perfect, so able and smart, the curiosity with which we blessed her led her to open Zeus's malevolent jar. To our horror, the evils contained so fragilely within it flew out into the world where they, even today, plague mankind."

Charis's head rose against Athena's deep breath.

"There is, however, one spirit—beautiful, bright, and pure—that yet remains in Pandora's Jar. Her name is Elpis, or as you would call her in your language ... Hope."

Charis leaned toward the waters of the stream that sparkled at the mention of Elpis's name. In them, a lone light, shaped like a tiny, winged woman, shone in the darkness. Athena quoted Hesiod's poem *Works and Days*: "Only Hope was left within her unbreakable house; she remained under the lip of the jar, and did not fly away before Pandora replaced the lid of the jar. This was the will of aegis-bearing Zeus the Cloud-gatherer."

"We gods believed that as long as Hope remained in the jar and in the possession of man, the balance of good and evil would survive. For eons that proved true. But in recent times, we are questioning our wisdom because evil runs rampant."

Athena passed her hands over the waters again. Pictures of recent wars, famine, and evil in many forms blazed upon the still surface. "The balance of the world is tilting ..."

"Why ... why are you showing me this?" Charis interrupted, a hint of fear quaking in her voice.

Athena rose from the grass and lifted Charis by the hands. "Let's walk, child."

As they strolled through the sunny garden, Athena continued her story.

"Charis, after Pandora released the spirits of evil into the world, the fate of man was forever changed, but it was a fate of the gods' making, and not man's. Man is not ultimately responsible ... we are."

"Well, can't you do something about it? You are gods, right?" Charis asked, surprised by her frustration. "I mean, what tha? Can't you just capture the evil and trap it again? This time in a stronger jar ... that no one can open?"

"How I wish we could! But, no, we can't. The gods are undeniably responsible for creating the evil. But man, or in this case *wo*man, is responsible for its release and *all* of mankind for its continued practice. Because a human set evil free, a human must also liberate its remedy. A human must also set Hope free from Pandora's Jar. That is where you come in, Charis."

Athena stopped walking and looked directly at Charis.

"Charis, there is a legend, one known only among the gods and not shared with the scribes for mankind's ears. I am going to tell you about it now. I need you to pay attention."

Charis nodded.

"Very well. Sometime after the release of evil, the Fates came to visit the gods in Zeus's temple at Mt. Olympus.

Charis wished they were still by the stream so she could see what Athena was describing.

"They grieved over the evil Zeus had made possible and rebuked him for interfering with the natural course of mankind. Zeus listened quietly and with great respect. Even the gods bow to the Fates, Zeus included. After scolding us all, they confessed that they knew all along of our hideous mistake and told us of a prophecy given them long ago by the Universe, before the earth was even formed."

"They said there would be born another woman, chosen by the hands of destiny, who could undo the damage we'd done. They said this woman alone matched the one attribute that led Pandora to open her jar, her curiosity. But unlike Pandora, who Zeus created with bad intentions, this woman was created with the purity of hope. They told us that, in addition to being smart and inquisitive, she would also bear the mark of Hermes, the Messenger God, because her birth brings the message of good news to man. They said she would have wings."

The birthmark in the middle of Charis's shoulders came alive, buzzing and tingling with sensation. She instinctively reached back to soothe it.

"The gods have spent years looking for both the jar, missing since Pandora first opened it, and the coming of the only girl child fit to open it. At last, we have found both the jar and the child."

Athena held Charis's hand once more and before the girl's eyes flashed images of her life. She saw her shiny soul floating in the sea of eternity before she was even born. It was wise and purposeful, pure and beautiful. The current guided her soul into the shared bright hope of her mother and father whose prayers mingled with Fate to bring her into the world. First breath. First steps. Everyday love calling her, beckoning her, preparing her for this moment in the garden with Athena.

"Charis, you are that child. It's you we've been searching for."

Like a flower blooming for the first time, Charis felt her destiny unfold, open, and spring to life within her heart. Charis moaned as her knees buckled beneath the weight of the immense burden now placed on her narrow, thirteen-year-old shoulders. Charis Parks, the only hope for her world.

Charis snatched her hand away from Athena's and clutched it to her chest. Questions flooded her mind, as did the cascading memories of every time she'd imagined just this moment. Ever since she could remember, Charis had fantasized that her birthmark *meant* something. She had always wondered at the moments when it created a sensation on her skin. When it itched, was it in anticipation? When it burned, was it with desire? She had always thought so, but it had never made sense. Until, possibly, right now.

But, this was a dream.

"I don't know what you're talking about. What are you saying, Athena?" Charis suddenly realized how ridiculous this was. She just called the figment of her imagination standing before her a name. She called her "Athena," as in "The Greek Goddess of Wisdom." She did this as naturally as if she were calling the name of her mom or dad. It was too much. From the safety of her warm bed, Charis's body began to struggle itself awake.

"Wait, Charis!" Athena urged, sensing she didn't have much longer. "Not yet ... you must stay here! There is more, much more I have to tell you. You are in danger!"

Danger?

Somewhere in the distance, beyond the dream, Charis moaned and cried. Within the garden, the verdant landscape surrounding her grew gray and brown and crumbled into abyss like clumps of ash. Leaves surrendered their proud places on the trees and hurled their shriveled, brittle bodies to the ground. Bullying black clouds pushed away the sun and blanketed the blue sky with threats. Birds that sang songs of hope shrieked their warnings of the unknown future. And Athena, lovely Athena, stood fading away before Charis's eyes, her light rapidly dimming into darkness.

"Athena!" Charis cried through sobs. "What's happening?" Her voice shook like the quaking ground beneath her.

Athena smiled weakly and lifted her proud head. "Until tonight, Charis." And then she was gone. Vanished.

Charis woke in a panic. The dream stuck to her just like her pajamas, wet with perspiration.

CHAPTER 12
A RUDE AWAKENING

CHARIS SAT UP IN HER BED with a jolt. "Ouch," she said, jamming her finger against her lamp as she reached through the dark. In her fumbling, she knocked Nike to the floor from the nightstand where the little goddess had watched Charis all night. Charis turned on the light and looked at the clock. 5:30 a.m. Exasperated, she flopped back onto her pillow and closed her eyes. She wanted to remember. Everything.

There was the hall or something. Some mirrors ... lots of mirrors. And, fog. What was the word? Special? No, chosen. Chosen! There was a door into a garden. What a garden! So green and fruitful, so beautiful ... beautiful. Athena!

Charis snapped back up again.

Athena. A stream. Mr. P. Zeus. Pandora. Evils. Hope. Fates. Me. ME?! The words flowed like a torrent in her thoughts.

Charis jumped out of her bed and ran to her dresser mirror. She craned her neck, searching for her birthmark. It was still there, her "Mark of Hermes."

Charis sat on the edge of the bed and shook her head full of curls. It was, clearly, a dream.

But it felt so real.

Charis rubbed her throbbing temples. Her head hurt from crying.

Why was I crying?

At once she remembered the last thing Athena said to her. She was in danger. Charis drew her knees to her chest and hugged them close.

Danger?

Charis went back and forth between explaining away the dream and trying to make sense of it. Information. She needed information. Charis went to her computer to begin her search. She bit her fingernails down to nothing as she read all she could find on Athena, Zeus, Pandora, and the Fates. She studied *Works and Days* with renewed interest, looking for clues or anything logical to cling to. As if that were even possible.

"Oooooooouch!" she whined, rubbing the knee she banged against her desk. The sudden buzzing of her alarm clock had scared Charis so good that she nearly jumped out of her seat. She shook her head at her nervous paranoia. 6:30 a.m. With a throbbing head *and* knee, she limped to the bathroom to get ready for the day.

After her shower, Charis stood dripping in front of the foggy mirror like she'd done every morning, but this morning felt different from any other. As she recalled the mirror from her dream, her word today felt more important than it ever had before. It felt serious ... a little scary too. What if when she wrote on the mirror her word disappeared and ...

Oh, don't be silly, Charis. It was a dream.

Charis reached up to the mirror with a tentative finger. "Seeker." That was it. That was her aim for the day, to be a seeker of truth. There had to be a rational explanation for her dreams. Too much studying. Too much writing. Too much mythology. Too much English class. Too much Mr. P.

Charis stayed at the mirror a little longer than usual, half expecting the word she'd written to disappear and be replaced by another.

This is stupid.

Charis went to her room and quickly got dressed. She gave her mom some lame excuse before skipping breakfast and sprinting out the door. Charis wanted to talk with Mr. P before school started. He'd understand, the way he was so into Greek mythology and everything.

"Tell Gabe I'll meet him there!" Charis yelled to her mom as she left.

If she had not been in such a hurry, if she had stayed in the bathroom for just a moment longer, Charis would have seen her that her word did in fact disappear. She would have seen that in its place, "REVELATION" was written in bold letters before the cool air blew the mist away.

CHAPTER 13
SEEING IS BELIEVING

MR. P PREFERRED getting to the school early, before his students arrived. He enjoyed opening the windows of his classroom to let in the crisp morning air. The quiet gave him the solitude he had often longed for since leaving his home on Mt. Olympus. Ordinarily, he went to temple in the mornings to say his prayers and make his offerings. Now, on earth, he had to take the temple with him in his heart and find snatches of time to visit it there … like in the peaceful mornings before school.

Mr. Papadakis, or *Erichthonius*, as was his name under ordinary circumstances, sat at his desk with his eyes closed. The stream of sunlight beaming through his windows rewarded his presence and warmed his face. He got to school especially early this morning because he knew Charis would be here too. His mother, Athena, told him about her visit with Charis last night and they both expected her to follow her curiosity straight to him. He needed the time to think, to prepare, so that he might provide his student the answers she sought.

Athena told her son that she found Charis delightful, brave, and every bit of the legend spoken concerning her. Athena explained that she had shared the story of Pandora with Charis and had showed her the grave consequences poured out upon the earth since the jar's opening. She told him she'd gotten as far as revealing Charis's true identity before fear had gripped the girl and snatched her from her dream. Athena regretted being unable to warn Charis of the Erinyes Sisters and of the despicable ploy discovered by Nike for Alecto to penetrate her realm posed as an art curator. The frightened look on Charis's face filled Athena with remorse as Eos, Goddess of the Dawn, lifted Charis away from sleep. Athena hadn't the chance to tell her she wasn't alone, but that the gods were with her to help in the task at hand.

Mr. P opened his eyes at the soft rapping on his classroom door. "Come in," he called.

Charis timidly poked her fuzzy head through the door.

"Hi, Mr. P," she said shyly.

She suddenly felt far less brave and sensible than she did during her run to see him. Was she really about to talk to her teacher—her *substitute* teacher—about a dream? If she didn't think she would die of embarrassment she would have turned around and dashed back home. Instead, she entered into the classroom, still breathing heavily. Charis flopped into a chair and tried to remember what she had rehearsed saying.

"Charis," Mr. P said, interrupting her thoughts. "What brings you here so early? Everything okay?" His raised eyebrows asked the question along with his words.

Charis took a long drink from her water bottle and then fumbled with it in her hands. "Sure, everything is fine ... I guess." As soon as she said the words she took them back.

"No, wait. Mr. P, everything is *not* fine. Or, at least, I'm not sure if it's fine." She shook her head. "Oh, geesh. I'm not making any sense."

"Take your time, Charis." Mr. P limped from behind his desk and sat next to her. "What is it?"

She took a deep breath. "Okay, this is going to sound crazy, but I had the most bizarre dream last night. It's one that I've been having almost every night lately, but this one was different. I mean, I remember it better than the others. And, I'm telling you about it because you were kind of in it."

She looked at his face, looking for a tell, a sign that he might have already known this. There wasn't one.

"Go on," he said.

"Okay, so I was in this hall; it was kind of like a museum or an opera house or something. It was beautiful and light was shining everywhere. And, the whole time I'm walking down the halls, I'm not really walking. I'm *floating*. That part is actually pretty cool," she chuckled. "Anyway, there's usually these pictures in the dream too. I don't know the people in them, but they try to talk to me and tell me things. This time, though, there were mirrors ..."

Charis stopped herself. She didn't want to tell Mr. P about her ritual with the mirror, so she moved on.

"But that's not important. What *is* important is that this time in my dream there was a door." Her hands got sweaty when she remembered how nervous she was to open it so she ran them across her jeans.

"It opened to this beautiful garden, and I mean beautiful. I've never seen anything like it in my life! Everything was just so perfect and green and sweet smelling. But that wasn't the best part about the garden. The best part about the garden was the woman who was in it. If she was a woman ..." Her voice trailed off and so did her thoughts toward Athena.

Danger.

The cool water felt good in her cotton mouth as Charis took another drink from her water bottle. Her heart beat faster sitting with Mr. P and telling him about her dream than it had when she was running.

"She said her name was Athena. Can you believe that? Athena?"

Mr. P kept his face neutral, waiting to hear the rest of Charis's story.

"Yeah ... we introduced ourselves and that's when she told me that she already knew who I was. She said you'd already told her about me." She stalled. "That's ridiculous, right? I mean, it's just a dream. Right?"

Before he could answer her, she blurted out what she hoped was the correct response. "Of course it is. It's ridiculous! I'm just being ..."

"Informed," Mr. P interjected. "You're just being informed, Charis." His eyes were soft, sympathetic, and watching for what would come next.

Charis sat, puzzled, with a frown on her face. *Informed?* When she finally made sense out of what he said, a quiet "What tha?" escaped her lips.

"Charis, I need you to listen to me." Mr. P held her hands, and just as they had with Athena, Charis's eyes opened. *Eternally* opened.

"Charis, it wasn't a dream, not in the way you think of a dream. It was real. Athena, my beloved mother, she visited with you. What she told you is real and true. You are the lone hope for your world. For both our worlds."

Charis gasped. She knew in an instant that everything he said was true ... that everything Athena said was true. She saw herself struggling against powers and spirits, against doubt and fear, to fulfill a destiny she hadn't even known was hers. In her mind's eye, she witnessed the darkness within the world grow and ultimately overcome all that which is good should she fail.

Charis snatched her hands away from his, hoping that if she could no longer see the inevitable, then it would go away. It didn't. Whatever gripped her while holding Mr. P's hand now had a hold on her heart. She had stared truth in the face and didn't like what she saw.

Like I could actually save the world. This is bonkers. I'm nothing ... special.

Charis sprung up on shaky legs and knocked her chair to the ground.

"What are you saying, Mr. P? What are you talking about? Athena's your mom? Are you crazy? Wait, maybe *I've* gone crazy! How do you know about my dream?"

Charis reached for her backpack, ready to run before anything else could burst free from her lips. For once, she wished she didn't have to ask so many questions.

Mr. P reached out, hoping to stall her.

"Don't! Don't touch me again! I swear!" Her voice was near hysterical.

"Wait, Charis. Just wait, please. I can prove it. I can prove that what I am saying is true, even though it might be hard to believe." Mr. P remained calm, hoping Charis would follow his example.

The voice in her head said to leave, but the deeper, quieter voice of her heart said to stay. She knew Mr. P was speaking the truth; she'd seen it, felt it. The dream was far too frequent and last night's was far too real to be ignored. The eye-opening, hand-holding thing couldn't be denied either. And, the place between her shoulder blades where her birthmark lived itched like crazy. Still, Charis wanted something more concrete.

"Prove it! Prove it then!" she insisted.

Mr. P walked with his uneven gait to the door and closed it. "Sit," he said limping back toward her. She eyed him warily as she picked up her chair and sat down on its edge. She was ready to bolt if she had to. Mr. P told Charis about the remainder of the dream and recited, word for word, all Athena said to her. Charis's eyes began to water.

"Why did she say I was in danger? What's going to happen to me?"

"Nothing. Nothing's going to happen to you, Charis. We're going to see to that. It is your destiny to find Pandora's Jar and open it. You were born, Child of Grace, to release hope into this world."

Mr. P told Charis about the tormenting Erinyes Sisters, and Alecto's plan to get the jar from the Getty.

"Charis, there are gods and imps alike who will stop at nothing to keep you from achieving your purpose, and we're not exactly sure why yet. That is the danger Athena warned you about. It's not an easy task ahead, and you will have to overcome much fear and doubt if you're going to succeed. But, you have help in the heavens and here on earth. I assure you, we will aid you in every way."

Charis wiped at her eyes, but they kept right on crying. There was an Alecto creature coming to her house for dinner. She wanted to warn her mom, to tell somebody, but she couldn't. What would she say anyway? Charis found herself needing to trust in gods who, until this very moment, were only alive in myths and fairytales, on parchment and paper.

This couldn't be happening. She thought about angry gods and what they might do to her and her family, and she felt helpless. But, then she thought about what Mr. P had said about helping her. He had said "we."

"Mr. P," she asked when her throat finally loosened enough so she could speak. "Who are you? Really."

"My name is Erichthonius. I *really* am Athena's son."

According to the myth, Hephaestus, the same god who fashioned Pandora, attempted to have his way with Athena. She successfully resisted his unwanted advances, so instead of impregnating the goddess, Hephaestus impregnated the earth. From the soil, Erichthonius was born and Athena raised him as her own. The baby was born lame, like his father … but in a much more distinct way. The child was born with the tail of a serpent. Charis knew the story like the back of her hand. Mr. P saw the look of recognition on Charis's face.

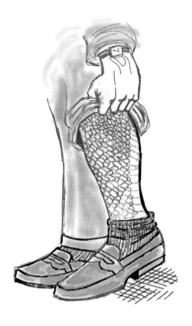

"Well, would you like to see it? My leg?" Mr. P asked. He knew she did.

Against her best judgment, Charis nodded, gripping the sides of her chair. Mr. P lifted his left pant leg and, though she wished she didn't, Charis saw serpentine flesh, shiny and thick, with blue, green, and black scales where his leg should be. Charis, the Child of Grace and hope for her world, then rose up from her seat and slowly fainted to the ground.

CHAPTER 14
(Un)Welcome

NIKE LAY STILL ON THE FLOOR until the house was empty before flying from beneath Charis's nightstand. The girl had left this morning in such a hurry that she'd forgotten all about her. The little goddess brushed herself free of dust bunnies and buzzed her way to the top of Charis's bed to survey the room. By now, she figured, Charis had made her way to school and, if she guessed correctly, was speaking to Erichthonius about her dream. Nike could tell by Charis's mumbling through the night that she was with Athena. She also knew, based on Charis's frantic Internet search, quick shower, and hurried departure, that she had remembered the dream for the first time. It was a good thing, too. Time was running dreadfully short if they were going to get the jar.

Nike wished she could be there when Charis met with Erichthonius. It would have been good to show her how supported and protected she is by the gods. As it stood, the goddess found herself walking ankle-deep across the plush quilt on Charis's bed deciding what to do with her time. She knew that if Erichthonius needed her, he could communicate that with just a thought.

Athena cautioned them about communicating with each other too carelessly though, especially in daylight hours. It was risky. The same energy that allowed the gods to share thoughts and commune on the earth also disabled the thin veil that shielded them from full visibility to the humans here. If the veil was removed, so were their disguises and their ability to walk the earth relatively unnoticed. If history taught anything, it was that gods discovered living among men could be tricky if not outright dangerous. Nike didn't know if Erichthonius, or "Mr. P," was with students or alone, so she thought better of contacting him. Still, she felt odd not being near Charis, her assignment.

The little goddess decided she'd take a flying tour around the house to pass the time. It would be prudent to get the lay of the land in case ever she had to defend it. She flew up to Charis's bookcase. It was cluttered with the prized possessions of her young heart. Little shiny trinkets dotted the shelves. Half-full, pink bottles of perfume and lotions crowded together. There were several framed pictures of Charis, Gabe, and Andy in various settings but always the same order: Charis in the middle, Andy to her right, and Gabe on her left. Nike flew toward the books. Worn school notebooks with crinkled pages and broken spines slumped in their places. There were also books of poetry, fiction, math, and yes, even mythology.

As she was about to venture downstairs, Nike heard a commotion that set her blood ablaze. She only ever got this feeling when trouble was near and a battle right behind it. She glowed deep red.

Nike unsheathed the sword that hung from her hips and flitted toward the window to investigate. When she got there it was as she suspected. Looking below, her blazing ruby eyes spotted Alecto.

So, it's begun.

Nike thanked Zeus that Charis had left her behind this morning.

The smoky figure below blew itself into Charis's house and disappeared from view. Nike quietly flew to the top of the stairs, listening. Downstairs she heard the rustling of Alecto's wings.

"Here we are," Alecto whispered in her mousy voice, so unaccustomed to making sound. "We are here ..."

The snakes on her head hissed their excitement in response.

Yessssss. Yessssss. Yessssss.

There was more rustling about. Nike descended the stairs slowly to see if she might get a glimpse of the malevolent intruder. She winced as the smell of the Underworld's decay rose from Alecto and filled the air as she drew closer. Slowly, Alecto came into view. Her presence felt big and consuming in the smallness of the room. The sunshine coming through the windows fought to have a place against Alecto's darkness. She was huge here. If she expanded her black wings they surely would have reached from wall to wall. For the first time, Nike became aware of her own miniature size.

Easier to maneuver, she reminded herself.

Alecto clumsily moved through the room. Every heavy footstep threatened to crash through the dark wood floors. Her ashen hands grabbed a photograph of Charis's family from the mantle above the fireplace.

"This mussst be the girl," she whispered, her razor-sharp fingernails tapping the glass. The snakes hissed once again. Their disapproval was venomous. Alecto hated this child, and she had good reason to.

When the gods found Charis, celebration filled the halls of Mt. Olympus. Even Zeus was grateful. He felt somewhat relieved of his guilt for booby-trapping the jar, so he lifted a toast to the girl's discovery. Hades didn't think much about it himself, until he found the jar that is. When Hades found the jar and understood how keeping it could benefit him and his kingdom, he took a keen interest in Charis and how he might stop her from ever opening it.

From the moment he drew lots with his brothers Zeus and Poseidon for control of the world, Hades was resentful. Zeus won the heavens *and* the title King of the Gods. Poseidon won dominion over the waters and seas. And, Hades, unlucky as he is, was relegated to the dark of the Underworld, a place that both man and god did their best to avoid. As King of the Gods, Zeus paraded around his heavens, throwing thunderbolts and tantrums at his whim while Poseidon swam his seas, toying with man and the ships he sailed. Hades, on the other hand, stayed underground, ruling over mostly miserable people in miserable circumstances. The only real pleasure he found was in the occasional treasure buried in the earth that was his to claim. Thus it was with Pandora's Jar.

About the jar, Hades believed what the other gods believed: as long as Hope remained entrapped within it, there was no hope for man and evil would continue to spread unchallenged. However, where the other gods were determined to find the jar and release its spirit of Hope, Hades was committed to keeping Hope imprisoned within the jar forever. After all, if mankind continued destroying himself, Hades's kingdom would grow. If his kingdom continued to grow, then maybe *he* would someday overthrow his pompous brothers and become King of the Gods himself.

As far as Hades was concerned, that was as it should have been from the beginning, and he would do all he could, including getting rid of this Charis person, to make it so.

In the privacy of his dark chambers, Hades told Alecto and her dreadful sisters about the Fates' prophecy and the girl, the "Grace." He explained that, yes, only the child could open the jar and free hope. But in *his* version of the story, if she did that, if Charis released Elpis and the spirit got away, then mankind was doomed and without any hope at all. In *his* version, the Fates told a cautionary tale and not a promising one.

"The girl," Hades warned, "the 'Grace' should be destroyed and not revered, not celebrated!"

This, of course, enraged the Erinyes Sisters completely. They lived to punish wrongdoers. And, in their minds, Charis was the biggest of all since Pandora opened the cursed jar so long ago. Their blood-red eyes flashed angrily as the snakes on their heads wailed their indignation!

What kind of monster must this little girl be?
Why would she rid her own kind of hope?
What evil must race through her very core?

They knew they had to stop her, to punish her. At all cost. Alecto and her sisters were entirely willing to do just that on behalf of Hades, their closest ally and only true friend among the gods!

Alecto slammed the picture frame back to the mantel. The glass cracked from the force.

"*The Grace*, indeed," she sneered.

She turned her horrible face toward the stairs. Alecto closed her eyes and took a deep breath through her long nose. She picked up Charis's scent and twisted her tiny mouth into a smile.

"Ssshall we go to the child's room?" The snakes on her head writhed and slithered with anticipation.

"I ssshall plant one of you beneath her bed," she sang. "You will be planted there for her."

Nike could hear the grin in her thread-thin voice.

"And when the time is right, you shall SSSTRIKE!" she cackled. *Yesssss. Yessssss. Yesssss.*

Nike quickly retreated back into Charis's bedroom and hovered behind the opened door, readying herself to attack when Alecto entered. She was small, but she could move fast to issue a fatal blow. As Alecto stalked up the stairs, Nike grew bolder and bolder with every groan of the staircase. Her whole body now shone silver and steel just like her resolve—just like her sword.

Alecto emerged, hunched, through Charis's bedroom door. Black, putrid dust orbited around her. The creature's back was to Nike. It would be a perfect strike. The Warrior Goddess raised her sword high above her head and prepared to descend into the twist and mangle of Alecto's snakes and through her skull. Nike darted forward at full speed but the unexpected sound of the garage door halted her attack, mid-air.

Alecto cocked her head and rambled awkwardly to the window. She saw the lady from the picture downstairs in a black car, waiting to enter into the garage.

"No!" she hissed. She could not get caught. She must not been seen. Hades would never forgive her or her sisters for another bungle. She had to leave. Before Nike's eyes, Alecto turned to ash and drifted out of Charis's opened window, a cloud of thick, black dust.

Nike sheathed her sword and flew to the window where Alecto had escaped. The little gold goddess knew that she would come back, and when she did, Nike would be waiting.

CHAPTER 15
KEEP CALM AND GO TO CLASS

"**CHARIS ... CHARIS ...** You okay?" Mr. P lightly tapped her cheeks.

When Charis opened her eyes she was surprisingly glad to see her teacher's familiar face. It meant she wasn't dead. Mr. P helped her to a chair.

"Here, take a drink."

"Thanks," she said, taking a sip of water and eyeing him suspiciously. Aside from a little wooziness, Charis felt fine. Well, as fine as one could feel having just learned that myths, while magical, are also factual; that her substitute teacher was a direct descendent of a god; and that if those things are true then dragons, unicorns, Excalibur, the Loch Ness Monster, and Santa Claus might be too.

She took a deep breath.

"Well, I'd say this is a bit awkward," she said timidly.

Mr. P smiled and nodded. He could only imagine what was going through her mind. Charis gazed down at his crippled leg. She couldn't deny what her eyes had seen.

"I can't believe I'm saying this, but let's assume I'm willing to believe this stuff is real. What do I do now?"

The morning buses had arrived and the voices of students filled the halls.

"You go to class," Mr. P said. "I'll see you next period, and it'll be business as usual. Come to my classroom during your lunch period and I'll fill you in on the things you need to know." He rose from his chair.

"In the meantime, try not to worry. Everything is going to be okay. I swear," Mr. P said as he limped toward the door and opened it.

"I swear ... by Zeus." He winked his eye at Charis who rolled hers back at him.

Charis gathered her things and walked past the long table lined with the papier-mâché masks of gods and goddesses that the class had made for Friday's play. She looked at them as if for the first time and shrugged her shoulders.

"By Zeus," she said wryly on her way out the door.

The first bell hadn't rung yet, so Charis went to the lunch tables where she and Gabe usually met Andy in the mornings. She stood on tiptoes to look over the students pouring into the campus, hoping she hadn't missed them. She really wanted to see their faces. She needed a bit of normal to her morning. So far, there had been nothing normal about it.

"What was the rush this morning?" Gabe asked from behind her. Charis turned around and, surprising even herself, grabbed him by the neck and hugged him tight, rocking him side to side.

"Okay, now I'm *really* curious," he said, narrowing his eyes. He couldn't suppress his smile though.

"Nothing," Charis lied, looking to the ground. "I just had to talk with Mr. P about the play. I had some ideas."

"About what?" Andy asked. Andy was met with a huge hug too. She and Gabe exchanged questioning looks behind Charis's back.

"Nothing. The play. It was nothing. We can talk about it later in class. Let's go." Charis didn't like lying to her friends, but she didn't know how she felt about telling them the truth either, or even if she should. The thought that Mt. Olympus just might be watching had crossed her mind.

Oh, brother ...

Gabe and Andy did most of the talking on the way to class. They went as far as they could before Andy left in the direction of her first period.

"See you next period, losers!" she shouted as she walked away.

Gabe continued to talk and Charis pretended to listen, his voice little more than background noise. Still, she was grateful that he was there beside her, familiar and real.

"Charis? Did you hear a word I just said?" Gabe asked, stopped in his tracks.

"What? No. No, I didn't. I'm sorry. What did you say?"

"Look. Are you okay? You've been acting really weird this morning. You leave your house early without even texting me. You hug Andy and me like, I don't know, like you haven't seen us in ages. And, you've hardly said anything this whole time, which is *totally* not normal. What's going on?"

If you only knew.

"Nothing. Promise. I just have a lot on my mind, that's all."

Business as usual is what Mr. P said. Business as usual. With a twinkle in her eye, Charis punched Gabe in his shoulder and took off running.

"Last one there has to raise their hand in class," she laughed, beating him to Algebra.

CHAPTER 16
HADES'S DISAPPEARING ACT

HADES'S DAILY DUTIES became little more than unwanted distractions. His dark mood was an added pox on the poor souls in his care. He felt bad about that, but it couldn't be helped. He sat on his throne, brooding and glum.

Hades had not heard from Alecto since her departure, "yesterday" in "people" time. How did their saying go? "No news is good news"? Something like that. He absentmindedly stroked Cerberus's heads as the beast sat dutifully beside him. The creature, massive and vicious as it is, had been subdued by some ill, black magic and rendered powerless to protect the jar when it was stolen. The defeat had demoralized it. It was shamed. Hades scratched its broad back in assurance. It wasn't to blame. He was. He should have been more careful with the jar.

Hades first discovered the jar when he learned about a group of archeologists digging in Lebanon's rocky terrain. As with every excavation site, Hades visited the dig from beneath the earth. He liked to get to the sites first to see if there were artifacts he should remove before the humans discovered them.

Given that he was Lord of the Underworld, Hades was the guardian of treasures buried underground. The gods depended on him to keep dangerous or magical relics away from the humans who were constantly in search of them. When a magic piece of antiquity escaped Hades's watchful eyes and ended up in the hands of man, invariably there were land disputes, lawsuits, and other squabbles among the humans for ownership. The gods hated when that happened. Already responsible for so much bickering among mankind, the gods did what they could to prevent more.

When Hades arrived in Lebanon, he could hardly believe his eyes. There it was, Pandora's Jar. It was as beautiful as he remembered. Hephaestus had never made anything more amazing—except, of course, for Pandora herself. Hades knew he should have told at least his brother Zeus about his find, but he had other, more self-serving ideas— ideas that were now in jeopardy if he didn't get the blasted jar back.

The disgruntled god had yet to find out who had made off with the jar, and he had to be careful in his investigation of the matter. He shouldn't have had it in the first place and could claim no legal ownership of it. If he went around interrogating every soul who had access to his Underworld, it would only raise suspicions. Hades didn't want the added attention. That would not be good. But, who had stolen it?

Taken it, his conscious reminded him, *it was never "yours."*

"Oh, shut up," Hades said aloud to himself.

He thought about who could possibly be responsible. Persephone, Hades's seasonal wife, had neither the opportunity nor, did he think, the reason to commit such thievery. According to Zeus's decree upon their marriage, Persephone had not left Hades's kingdom at all, given that it was the winter months. And it was during this, her assigned time to remain in the Underworld, that the jar had gone missing.

Charon, the faithful ferryman of the river Styx, never, ever left his post. The ghostly seaman was too greedy to leave his ferry and miss out on the coins paid to him by his newly deceased passengers crossing death's dark river.

Then, there were the Erinyes Sisters. Truly, Hades could conceive of no circumstance in which they would benefit from taking the jar. They stood to gain nothing in its disappearance and had been eager to assist him in its retrieval once he told them of his plight.

Your fictitious plight, his conscious challenged. *Your "concern" for the future of man. Ha!*

"Oh, shut up," Hades said once more.

Hades did feel some remorse in deceiving the Erinyes Sisters about why he had the jar in the first place, but it could not be helped.

He had only said what he must to secure their assistance and loyalty. So what if he embellished the prophecy a bit for his own gain? He needed the jar back. A human girl child was not going to stand in the way of his grand schemes. It didn't matter whether she was innocent or not. He had to make the Erinyes Sisters hate her, and hate her they did.

Their devotion to ending the little girl frightened even Hades. He had never seen anyone as committed to a single cause as the Erinyes Sisters were to Charis's destruction. He, Lord of the Underworld, shuddered at the thought of ever being the recipient of their unrelenting wrath. He would have felt pity for the girl had he not been so focused on his own agenda. She was surely no match for the Erinyes Sisters and was only a hapless consequence. It could not be helped.

No, no. It wasn't the sisters.

Hades's blood ran cold when, at last, he remembered Hermes.

Oh, Hermes … The fair Messenger God, beloved by all. Pah!

He curled his hands into fists at the thought and beat them down on the armrests of his throne. The sound sent shockwaves into the atmosphere and feckless cries from unknown places rose into the air. Sensing a change in its master's mood, Cerberus slunk away from Hades's reach and into the dark.

Hermes.

The god was always flying in and out and in and out of the Underworld, guiding newly dead souls to their new eternal abode. Hermes alone had the kind of freedom and access that would enable such a theft.

But why? Why would he take it?

Stroking his thick, black beard, Hades knew that Hermes could ask him the very same question, thus the dilemma.

Hermes hadn't given anything away. His words, always heard *and* felt, were nothing more than neutral. The winged god gave no signs of guilt. He maintained his scheduled visits and performed his duties as if nothing had happened.

Hades lifted his well-chiseled body from this throne and walked toward a beautiful, gold cabinet, sealed with a lock only he could release. He whispered secret words into it and the doors glided open.

There, on the single shelf inside, sat the Helm of Darkness, the weapon given him during the War of the Titans. It gave him the gift, or *curse*, of invisibility. He lifted the helmet to his head and sat it atop his generous, black curls. Hades disappeared and laughed, his voice coming from nowhere.

"I'll get to the bottom of this," he promised.

His footsteps fell and echoed into the darkness he had become.

CHAPTER 17
SEEING IS BELIEVING...
FOR REAL THIS TIME

FINALLY. LUNCHTIME. Charis's morning English class with Mr. P was just weird, and electric. Each group was busy putting the finishing touches on their projects for the play. Kids ran around with paint in one hand and cardboard in the other. The lead kids stood in corners reciting lines and making over exaggerated hand gestures. The chorus kids huddled together, dramatically rehearsing their narration and trying to synchronize their moves just right. The playwrights went from group to group, lending a hand wherever one was needed since the script was already finished, at last.

Ordinarily, Charis would have been psyched about all of the action, but today Mr. P was the sole object of her attention. She just couldn't take her eyes off of him. It was as if Brady wasn't even in the same room. Charis had so much she wanted to ask Mr. P, and lunchtime couldn't come soon enough.

When the lunch bell rang after third period, Charis made up some random reason to excuse herself from Gabe and Andy before sprinting to Mr. P's room. She found the door opened when she got there.

"Charis!" he said, cheerily. "Come in!"

Charis slumped in the chair she toppled earlier and stared into Mr. P's face. She was slightly annoyed that he was smiling.

"Okay, Mr. P, no beating around the bush. Let's start from the beginning. The *beginning* beginning." Charis twirled her hair around her fingers like she did every time she was nervous.

"What like, in the beginning ... God?" he asked.

"No, no ..." but then she thought about it. "You could do that?"

Charis sat upright and at attention. She might finally be given the ultimate answer to the question of Why. Plainly. She bit her lip in anticipation.

Mr. P laughed out loud and slapped his leg. The human one.

"I could, but that's already been done, Charis. Many, many times and by many, many saints and sages alike. What do you say we start with *your* beginning, shall we?"

Mr. P retold her what she already knew. Prometheus's theft. Zeus's trickery. Pandora's Jar. The curse on mankind. The prophecy of the Fates. The birth and discovery of her, the Grace.

"So, how did you find me? Here? Now?"

"The stars. Signs of the times. Facebook."

Mr. P explained that ever since the Fates had prophesied about Charis, Athena and Hermes had monitored the heavens and the earth looking for her, the Grace. He said that there were many false alarms in the years which followed, with near countless sightings of girl children who may or may not have been Charis. Each time the gods thought they'd found her, the child would be lacking in some way.

"But with wars escalating and diseases spreading like wild fires among men, we knew it wouldn't be long until mankind had only two ways to go—total destruction or renewed salvation. It helped that the stars were aligned with our deductions and all but pointed the way to here and now. To you."

"But ... Facebook? What tha?" Charis asked.

"Ah, the wonders of technology! You know, even the gods are impressed with man's inventions here lately. You all are absolutely *full* of beautiful and terrible possibilities." He paused to sigh. "Beautiful and *terrible*, indeed."

"Anyway, about Facebook, your pictures caught our attention. The ones you posted of you and your family at the beach revealed your mark, the Mark of Hermes. When we saw those, I came here to the earth to meet you, to help you."

Charis's head was swimming. Gods checking out Facebook? It was too much. She wanted to know more, to know everything. She couldn't help it. Mr. P knew this; however, there simply wasn't time to tell her all that he could.

"Charis, I know you have questions … *lots of them* … but there are some urgent things you need to know now. These next few days are vitally important and you've much to learn."

Mr. P told Charis about Hermes finding the jar in Hades's possession. He explained how Hermes took it and gave it to him to discretely place among the other antiquities at the Getty Museum, making it accessible to Charis.

"Okay, so this sounds simple enough, right?" Charis asked. "I just need to get to the jar and open it. I'll be at the Getty on Friday, you know."

Of course he knows. He probably knows everything about me.

"It might *sound* simple, but I'm afraid it's not. It's pretty complicated, and dangerous."

That's when Charis remembered Athena's warning. She twisted another lock of hair and braced for the bad news.

"Don't worry, Charis," Mr. P said, watching the tip of Charis's finger turn white from the lack of circulation. "When I said you have help in fulfilling your destiny, you do."

Mr. P told her the truth about that dazzling keychain she found in her backpack a few days ago. Charis quickly patted her hips and discovered it wasn't there.

"That's … um, *she's* Nike? As in the Goddess of Victory, Nike? Titan war, Nike?" Charis could hardly believe it.

"The very one," Mr. P assured.

"I knew it! I knew something was weird about that thing! I mean," she blushed, "about *her*. Something weird about *her*."

Charis remembered knocking Nike to the floor when she woke up, frantic from her dream. She suddenly felt very, very bad and slightly paranoid about it.

"Nike is your guide and protection," Mr. P said. "She's here to help and *protect* you too."

"Okay, okay, Mr. P. Enough with the secrets already. Protect me … from what?" she asked. The lump that formed in her stomach struggled to make its way into her throat.

Mr. P told her about the Erinyes Sisters conspiring with Hades to retrieve the jar, and how they had almost been successful in their first attempt.

"Luckily, fate intervened," he said. "We were most grateful, but also saddened. We think there may have been a human casualty."

Charis shuddered in spite of the turtleneck she wore.

"Charis, as I said this morning, we now know for sure that Alecto is either coming to the earth or is here already. She plans to pose as an art curator, a 'Mr. Al Ecto' to position herself close to you and the jar at the Getty Museum."

The hairs on Charis's arms stood up and the birthmark on her back blazed. Charis clutched her stomach. Waves of concern churned in her belly and she started to feel sick. The Erinyes Sisters were those crazy creatures who went around tormenting people for their crimes … often to the point of making them commit suicide.

Oh, God!

And one of them, Alecto, is coming to her house for dinner … to kill her … and possibly her family … and possibly her Gabe.

Oh, GOD!

"Mr. P?" Charis finally asked, risking vomiting. "Does this mean my mom didn't get the Getty account, fair and square, because she worked hard for it? Does this mean she got it because I'm some weird girl starring in some stupid prophecy? Because if that's what has happened, she'll be *so* bummed!"

"No, no, Charis," Mr. P said, struggling to suppress a smile. "We did not intervene there. Your mother's great. That was very lucky for us."

Ridiculous as it was, Charis actually felt better and let go of the balled up sweater in her fist. At least she wouldn't have to deal with Alecto *and* her mom.

"Charis," Mr. P said as the lunch bell rang. "When you get home and can have a private moment with Nike, she'll be able to tell you more. For now, just go on with your day as normally as you can."

"Seriously? Normally?" Charis huffed, looking heavenward.

"Yes, seriously. Please," Mr. P softly answered. "As difficult as it will be, you must. Can you do that?"

"Sure. Okay. I mean … fine. I'll try."

"That's all I ask. Now, you'd better get going. We don't want to raise any suspicions, now, do we?"

Mr. P walked Charis to the door. His limp was almost invisible to her now. She still couldn't help but stare down at his leg though.

"Can I see it? Again?" She thought it would make her believe more and settle things in her head and heart once and for all. Plus, it was kind of cool in a freaky way.

"You're going to see greater wonders than this. Trust me."

Mr. P lifted his khaki pant leg and the wet-looking blackish and bluish scales that sent Charis fainting to the floor earlier were still there. Instead of falling down this time, she knelt down to touch it. The scales were slick and bumpy beneath her touch. It was real. This all was. She wouldn't doubt it again.

Though Charis may not have doubted her eyes, Gabe sure did. Because Charis had been acting so strange, Gabe followed her after she ditched him at lunch. From behind the classroom door, he watched in horror as Charis stroked the scaly thing that should have been Mr. P's leg. A wide-eyed Gabe would have screamed his head off had his hands not been stuck over his mouth like glue.

CHAPTER 18
PLEASED TO MEET YOU

CHARIS WAITED FOR GABE after school beneath California's perpetual sun. She impatiently shifted her weight from one foot to the other and back to the other again.

Where could he be?

"Of all days," she said to herself. Today was NOT the day Charis wanted to wait around. Andy had already given up on him for fear that she'd miss her bus.

"Tell Gabe I said 'peace,'" she said before sprinting off. "TTYL!"

Charis's afternoon classes had felt like obstacles to overcome and mountains to climb, each one standing in the way of her making it home to Nike. She had hardly paid attention to anything her teachers had said, her mind was so entirely elsewhere. Plus, she had barely even noticed when Lauren and the Harpies blocked her way to 5th period and inundated her with Jolly Jam-related fashion updates. Charis's blank stare seemed the talisman against their black magic because they quickly went about their merry ways.

The stream of kids leaving the campus trickled down to almost none and there was still no sign of Gabe. She texted him … again. This time, she heard his ringtone chirp behind her.

"There you are!" she said, exasperated. "Where've you been?"

"I had some stuff to do," he said half-heartedly. Gabe shifted his eyes from the ground to the sky to the plants to his feet to his hands to the …

"What's wrong? You okay?" Charis asked. "Want to talk about it?" She hoped not. She wanted to get home. Now.

Gabe finally let his eyes meet hers. "I don't know."

Charis raised an eyebrow. Her friend was clearly not himself, but she needed to get home because, as it turned out, she wasn't herself either. At least not the self she'd known for the past thirteen years.

"Well," she said reluctantly, "let's walk, and we can talk about it if you want."

Charis did her best to make normal conversation, but neither she nor Gabe had their hearts into it. They walked home in the kind of silence comfortable between friends. But that changed when they finally reached Charis's house. That's when that awkward kind of silence stepped in. Ordinarily, Gabe would follow Charis inside, they'd have a snack, do homework, help with dinner, watch some TV, and then he'd go home only to text her several times before bed. But today, they both just kind of stood there in front of her blue front door.

Charis knew why she was stalling; she wanted time alone with Nike. Her dad worked from home most afternoons, but that meant he'd be in his office out back. With him out there, Charis could talk as freely with Nike as she wanted until her mom and Presley got home. But, she had no idea about what was going on with Gabe or that agonizing look on his face.

What's he just standing here for? And, that's when it hit her.

"Gabe?"

He looked … sick.

"Tell me," she insisted. "What?"

"You tell me, Charis!" Gabe shouted before lowering his voice to an angry whisper. He spoke through pursed lips. "I've got a few questions of my own."

Gabe confessed to following Charis to Mr. P's class, then he barraged her with questions and accusations.

What's all this business with Mr. P? And, what kind of freak is he anyway? What were you talking about at lunch? You can't be serious with all of this Greek mythology stuff. Do your parents know you're freaking out? How could you keep something like this from me?

"And, seriously, Nike?" By now, Gabe's hair was a total mess. "I'm not going home, Charis," he said. "I'm coming into the house with you. You know I am."

"Fine," Charis huffed and pointed a finger in his face. "Fine, but if I get in trouble with ... with *them*, you're in trouble too! Got it?"

"Fine!"

Charis and Gabe composed themselves on the front porch before easing into her house. They each said a quick hello to Charis's dad before running upstairs to see Nike. They found the little goddess sitting on the edge of Charis's desk. She had overheard their conversation outside, so she wasn't at all surprised to see Gabe rubbing his head standing next to Charis. On the other hand, the look of surprise on *their* faces made her laugh. She stood to her feet, and with her tiny, sparkly little body lighting up the whole room, Nike greeted them in the voice of a thousand angels.

"Charis, Gabe, I am Nike."

The two friends bolted to the dresser and slid to their knees. Nike stood eye level before them.

"Holy. Freakin'. Crap!" Gabe blurted.

Charis frowned and punched him in his shoulder.

"Keep it down! And, dude. Holy? *Crap*? Really?"

"Sorry," Gabe mumbled, rubbing his shoulder. Nike stood there waiting for them to say something, ask a question, anything, but words had clearly escaped them.

"Wellllll, okay then," she said, breaking the silence. "Shall we get started?" Nike asked as she flew into the air.

Without waiting for a response, she motioned the two of them to the bed.

"Have a seat, you two."

She waited impatiently as Charis and Gabe stumbled forward, tripping over each other and not taking their eyes off of her. When they finally sat down, Nike hovered before them with her hands on her hips. Charis and Gabe stared, slack-jawed, at the goddess, exchanging glances and giggling nervously between them. Nike cleared her throat. She would be here forever waiting for these two to come around.

"All right," Nike sighed. "Enough. We haven't time for this."

In a burst of speed, Nike flew to the ceiling, in between Charis and Gabe, and all around the room. She changed colors from green to red to pink to gold to silver. All the while, she shouted from above, below, and in between them.

"This is real," she yelled as she zoomed by.

"I am here," in a flash.

"This *is* happening," fast as light.

Charis and Gabe whipped their heads around trying to keep up with her before she finally stopped in front of Charis's face.

"Charis Parks, we have work to do. Do you understand me?"

Speechless, Charis nodded a frantic yes.

"Okay then," Nike flew to Charis's desk and stood there. "We simply must press on." Nike paced back and forth, like a general addressing an army. "As you know, I've been sent here to protect you …"

"Um, no offense, Mrs. Nike ma'am," Gabe stammered. "But, how are you going to protect anyone? You're like … like five inches tall."

Gabe knew it was probably foolish to question a god, and so soon after just meeting her, but he couldn't help himself. Charis was his best friend, and if what he overheard in Mr. P's classroom about creatures coming to get her was true, then he wasn't sure some five-inch, figurine-looking little goddess was going to do the trick. Offending her was a risk he was willing to take.

"I'm *four* inches tall," Nike corrected him, halting her steps. "And I'm more than able to fulfill my purpose. Don't equate the smallness of my stature with the size of my will to live out my destiny."

In truth, Nike privately questioned her ability to protect Charis too, confined as she was within such a small body. But she would never let them know about her uncertainty. Nike wore her confidence like armor against the doubts that besieged her.

"No matter my form, I am the Goddess of Victory in every way."

The little goddess glowed redder with every word, as if to prove her point. Gabe took her rebuke and was grateful for it. At least that meant Charis was safe. His wounded pride was a small price to pay for that assurance.

Charis knew Gabe was worried about her. She was worried about her too. This was all so strange and unreal, until a few hours ago. For a girl who always wanted to know why, this was a leap into the unknown that she was scared to make. But, looking at a real-life Nike, even a small one, made her at least a little willing. Charis reached for Gabe's hand and squeezed it.

"Let's proceed," Nike instructed. "As Mr. P told you ... *both* of you," she said casting red eyes in Gabe's direction, "Alecto is certainly here. In fact, she breached your home earlier today, Charis."

Charis gasped and squeezed Gabe's hand tighter.

"She didn't know I was here, so I was able to discover her plan of attack. As fate would have it, we were very fortunate that you left me here today, Charis."

"What ... what did she try to do?" Charis stuttered.

Nike told her about Alecto's head full of snakes and her intention to leave one in Charis's room. Charis didn't need her to explain why or what for. She got it. She looked at Gabe with tears in her eyes.

"I'm scared, Gabe. I'm scared. I didn't ask for any of this. I swear I didn't." She couldn't stop herself from sobbing any longer. All this talk about being *special*, being *chosen,* wasn't all it was cracked up to be. In fact, normal looked pretty amazing right now.

Gabe hugged Charis close but he looked straight into Nike's eyes the whole time.

"It's going to be okay, Charis," he said. *"It better be,"* is what he mouthed to Nike.

Nike changed her color to a soothing shade of blue.

"Charis. Gabe is right. It will be okay. I swear ..."

"I know, I know ... by Zeus" Charis said, hoping it meant something.

* * *

The rest of the evening passed as any other. Evan started a shrimp dinner. Presley arrived home smelling of the gym. Mona came in with a flurry of stilettos, mobile devices, and kisses for everyone, including Gabe. As for Charis and Gabe, the two of them pretended they had not just spent hours upstairs talking to the goddess who now hung from Charis's jeans at the waist.

The conversation over dinner was lively. Evan was excited about the Rose Bowl tickets he'd won at work and Presley was busy attempting to finagle them from him. In the middle of their ruckus,

Mona reminded everyone that, unlike tonight, she expected them to be on their best behavior tomorrow for Mr. Ecto's dinner. Charis's birthmark began to itch and both she and Gabe resisted the temptation to look down at Nike who remained a stoic picture of calm. Mona went over the details about how they were going to make this hellish creature from another realm as comfortable and honored in their home as possible.

Charis listened silently as her mother went on and on giving instructions about etiquette, the menu, and the like. She wanted to scream in protest, but couldn't. "You must not tell anyone else!" Nike had warned.

"Charis and Gabe, will you two share your play with Mr. Ecto?" Mona asked. "I'm sure he'll be thoroughly entertained hearing your version of Pandora's Jar. Won't that be great?"

Sigh.

After dinner, Charis walked Gabe to the door. "Be careful, okay?" she said. "Now that you know what's going on, I … I hope I haven't put you in any danger or anything." It would crush her if she had. She should have been more careful.

"I'll be fine," Gabe assured her, shoving her lightly on the shoulder to break the tension. And then, Gabe did something he had never done. The boy bent down and kissed Charis gently, slowly on the lips—like he had done it a million times before. Charis's eyes fluttered opened when he finally pulled away.

Before she could say anything, Gabe ran out the door and into the chilly, dark night.

WEDNESDAY

The greater the difficulty, the more the glory in surmounting it.

—EPICURUS

CHAPTER 19
DEBATING DESTINY

ALONG WITH ATHENA ...

Charis stood at the foggy mirror in her towel, her hair dripping wet. She read the words she'd written there and waited. Then, from beneath the fog, it came. Writing, embellished and beautiful, from an invisible finger.

... move also your hand.

Charis couldn't help but smile. Her time with Athena in last night's dream was incredible. They talked for hours. At least, that's what it felt like. And yet Charis was rested and feeling optimistic this morning. Charis couldn't wait to see Gabe to tell him about it. She knew that he was probably better off not knowing about any of this, but Charis was glad to have someone she could talk to, even if it complicated things. Her excitement lasted until she remembered what day it was: Wednesday. It was her mother's bustling downstairs that reminded her.

She overheard Mona on the phone with her assistant. *I'll forward my calls to you should I break for lunch. I've already logged into the network. No, but the caterers will be here at 4:00. Can you call to confirm? Don't forget the flowers. Yada yada yada.*

Charis clutched her stomach, hoping that would settle it.

Tonight was dinner. With Alecto. This was her lucky day.

She raised her eyes to the fading words on the mirror.

Along with Athena, move also your hand.

That's what this all came down to. As much help as the gods extended—snake-legged teachers to guide her, miniature goddesses to protect her—Charis knew that unless she actually did something and worked along with them to get the jar, it was useless. She could hope in them all she wanted, but at some point there were things only she could do. Namely, open the jar. After last night's talk with Athena, Charis understood this clearly.

Yes, the gods had made every provision for her success, but ultimately Charis had to trust them and to act upon that trust. They couldn't do this for her. Nor could they make her do it for them. They could only point the way, provide the help, and make the promises they hoped she believed. The journey to Pandora's Jar was Charis's alone to make, and hers alone to succeed or fail. Charis believed this is what faith felt like.

"Charis," Mona called. "Are you getting ready, babe?"

As soon as Mona's eyes opened, she hit the ground running. She regretted scheduling something as important as this dinner so close to the opening of *The Ancients Alive* exhibition, but everyone involved in the project was indebted to Mr. Ecto. His willingness to step in for that loafing Mr. Ward character saved the show and, in part, the reputation of her advertising firm.

"Charis?"

Charis skulked down the stairs, every step feeling like one closer to her doom. Her mom gave her a hug. "Hey, pretty girl," she said. Charis put a brave face on as her mother lifted it to kiss. "You good?"

"Yeah," she lied.

Charis pushed the floating cereal circles around in her bowl and ate very little. She was preoccupied with knowing that tonight could be her last meal. Soon, she'd be confronted with someone who wanted to … who wanted to … she couldn't bring herself to think it.

"You're awfully quiet, Sunny," Presley said, rousing her from her thoughts. "You a'ight?"

"Huh? Yeah. I'm good," she smiled. Another lie.

"Gabe's early this morning," Mona said looking at her watch as the doorbell rang. Charis figured he would be. He probably couldn't wait to ask her if yesterday was just a dream or if he really did talk with a four-inch Greek goddess about monsters and such.

"Don't forget. Come straight home after school today, okay? There's that dinner ..." Mona called as Charis walked out of the front door.

The day was overcast. Fitting for the gloom Charis felt in her chest. After they were a few steps away from the house, Charis pinched Gabe's arm. Hard.

"Oooowwww! What was that for?" he whined.

"That was for kissing me last night! What the heck was *that* for?"

"I don't know," he said rubbing his arm up and down. "I just got caught up in the moment, I guess. Damsel in distress. Knight in shining armor kind of thing. How'd I do?"

Charis thought back on the kiss and was surprised to find herself blushing. It was her first.

"You did alright, I guess. Geesh, how should I know? But you of all people know I'm no *damsel in distress*, and even if I was, I don't need a knight, I have a Nike."

"Speaking of, do I say hello to her or something?" He looked at Nike who was hanging from Charis's backpack. "I mean, I don't want to be rude."

Charis shrugged her shoulders.

Nearly imperceptibly, Nike shook her head no, frowning her brow.

"Okay, sorry," Gabe replied. They walked a little ways in silence. "How did you sleep last night?" Gabe asked. "Did you have that dream again?"

"Yeah," she said.

"And?" Gabe asked.

"And, it was great. I mean, talking with Athena is one of the coolest things ever. It's all this other stuff that's got me stressed."

"Well, what did she say about that Erinyes thing?" Charis watched him muss up his hair as he ran his hand over it.

"I don't even know why you bother combing it," Charis said, shaking her own head full of crazy hair. "She said a bunch of stuff. She said, 'Along with Athena, move also your hand.' She told me to try not to worry about anything, but to trust the gods to help me, to protect me. She wants me to trust them enough to do what they've asked me to do. She said that since the beginning, the gods have always worked with people in doing things in the world. This jar business would be no different." Charis stopped walking.

"Seriously, Gabe, what choice do I have? That Underworld freak is coming to my house whether I want her to or not." Charis raised her voice, and for the first time she realized she was angry and not afraid.

"I've got to deal with that. And, what am I going to do, act like Pandora's Jar doesn't matter? Why? So this whole freakin' world can go down the drain and us with it?" Charis slapped her hand to her forehead. "God! I feel so stupid even saying these things! Who the heck do I think I am?"

Charis looked around at her neighborhood. Mr. Moore lived in the brown and green house three doors down from Charis. Around four months ago, his wife had died of cancer and now he was raising their two small kids on his own. Charis and Gabe had made them cookies for the wake. The Clarks lived in the yellow and white house with the spotty lawn. Mrs. Clark called Charis's mom all the time, crying and worried about her son serving in the Middle East. And, the Thoms lived in the blue and gray house with the three-car garage. They looked like they had the perfect family, but Charis knew that their fourteen-year-old daughter Becca was up to things no kid her age should be up to. She couldn't believe the girl's parents couldn't see it.

Trouble. It was everywhere. Trouble. Sadness. Despair. Charis didn't have to look farther than her own best friend. She had noticed a long time ago that his eyes were just a little bit sadder since his parents' divorce.

Not that she'd asked for it, but all of the sudden it was up to Charis to give these people hope for their futures. It didn't seem fair, but fairness didn't matter. Nothing else mattered but the freakin' jar. Nothing. All that drama about the Jolly Jam dance seemed pretty dumb right now.

"Gabe, look, I can't follow 'destiny' *and* fear at the same time. It's one or the other. I'm scared out of my mind … *crazy* scared, but what choice do I have?" She grabbed both of Gabe's hands, not caring that hers were clammy with nerves. "Listen, if this is my destiny, then it's yours too because I know I can't do this without you."

"Don't worry, Charis. You won't have to. I promise you that," Gabe said, wanting to seal it with another kiss.

CHAPTER 20
ALECTO CHECKS IN

IT WAS A BRIEF, awkward exchange. The front desk clerk at the W hotel in Los Angeles couldn't get this guest checked in fast enough. He wanted him away, not that he hadn't encountered strange types before. This was LA after all. No amount of trendy decor could keep out *all* of the riffraff. But this dude grossed him out and gave him the heebie jeebies.

"Mr. Al Ecto, you said?" Through his puny mouth, the guest said "yes," though the clerk could hardly hear him. The young man unconsciously took another step back as he tapped on his keyboard with the very tips of his fingers looking for the reservation.

"Ah. Here you are, Mr. Ecto."

The clerk would ordinarily give his winning, I-wanna-be-a-Hollywood-star smile, but that meant looking at the guest standing in front of him. He had already made that mistake when the unnaturally tall man first lumbered up to the desk. The poor clerk felt a little uneasy ever since. He didn't know what bothered him most: the greasy, jet-black hair that moved like Jell-O on top of the dude's head, the grayish hue of his skin, or the faint smell of rot emanating from his ill-fitting clothes. The clerk wrinkled his nose and kept his eyes on the computer screen. His manager would be pissed if he saw him deliberately avoiding looking at this guest, but he couldn't help it.

To heck with customer service.

"I'll be right back, Mr. Ecto. I'm going to retrieve your room keys." Alecto nodded her long, crescent-shaped head. When the clerk turned his back to her, the hairs on his neck stood up. Yep, he had the creeps.

That dude is the creeps.

Behind him, Alecto impatiently rapped her yellowing fingernails on the surface of the counter.

"Here you are, sir."

The clerk slid the keys across the surface, careful not to touch Alecto's hands.

"Should you need anything, our concierge service is available 24/7."

The young man forced himself to look at Alecto's face, into her reddish, brown eyes. His underarms tingled with nervous sweat as he forced a smile on his face.

"As you know, there are many fabulous LA attractions surrounding our hotel. If you're interested in recreational fun, Disneyland isn't far. If you'd like to see one of our beautiful beaches …" though, he couldn't imagine Alecto's ashen skin had ever seen the sun… "the Santa Monica Pier is very close. Or, if art and culture are more your speed, the Getty Center is right up the way."

The clerk saw a smile fight its way onto Alecto's strange face. The pain of it made him glad this little encounter was nearing its end.

"If there is anything we can do to make your stay more comfortable, don't hesitate to let us know."

Alecto whispered something the young man couldn't make out.

"Pardon me, sir?"

"Don't disturb me," Alecto repeated. "Do not disssturb."

"Oh, no, sir. You'll find your room has already been made today. You needn't worry about housekeeping."

"No," Alecto said. Her patience was dangerously thin, like the sound of her voice, dangerous and thin.

"Ever. Don't disssturb me ever," Alecto warned.

"No problem there, sir. No problem there."

The clerk gratefully pointed Alecto to the elevators. She lumbered toward them, weighed down with the black, boxy luggage she refused to give to the porter. The smattering of other guests in the lobby parted before her like the Red Sea. They were inexplicably repulsed too.

As Alecto stood waiting for the doors to open, her dowdy drabness looked ridiculous against the chic cool of the hotel. When the doors finally opened and Alecto stepped inside, there was a collective sigh of relief from everyone and everything around her.

"And a good day to you too, weirdo," the clerk said to himself, taking a deep breath from the fresher air around him.

CHAPTER 21
DANCES AND DINNER DISASTERS

ENGLISH CLASS MET in the auditorium. They planned to perform a full dress rehearsal for Friday afternoon's show. When the class had first started the project, Charis was disappointed she didn't have a speaking role. Now that she could watch from the shadows and not the spotlight, she was grateful. She didn't much feel like having the spotlight today.

"Pretty cool, huh?" Andy said, interrupting Charis's thoughts. Andy grinned as she lifted her mask to her face. Although the toga hanging loosely around her body was uninspired, the mask rocked.

"I know I'm only a member of the chorus, but," she said cutting her eyes at the other chorus members, "my mask is the best of the bunch." She ran her fingers through the black yarn of hair. "It's all this fabulous, thick hair, I think. Don't you, dahling?" She dramatically swung her own thick ponytail that sat on top of her head. This was her "diva" move.

"You're so silly!" Charis laughed, grateful for the comic relief. "And, yes, your mask kicks some serious butt!"

"Places everybody," Mr. P shouted. "We don't have much time." He looked at the clock glowing red numbers above the heavy double doors. "In fact, we've even less time than I thought. Let's get going here."

"Gotta run. My adoring public awaits," Andy giggled.

"Break a leg!"

The excited chatter neared a hush as students took their places.

"Lights?" Mr. P said.

The kids helping from the theatre group dimmed the lights and everything went dark. Charis watched the action from the seats near the back of the auditorium. Gabe sat protectively beside her on one side, Nike on top of the backpack on the other.

"Enter chorus!" Mr. P directed.

From the back of the room, twelve masked students, six in each aisle, marched solemnly toward the stage. Their togas, dreadfully plain in comparison to Athena's, swept against the ground. Andy waved at Charis and Gabe as she passed by. Her mask really was the coolest. Together the chorus chanted the opening song, the parodos, as they made their way forward. Except, it wasn't really a song, it was more like a rap, which Mr. P was totally okay with. In one voice, they said:

"Here is the tale of tragedy and woe. Of fire, desire. Of tears, of sorrow. Prometheus, the Titan, with greed in his heart, from Olympus stole fire and a flame he did start. Igniting the wrath of the Lightning God, Zeus, who burned with revenge for the trickster Prometheus. Zeus commanded the gods a woman to create, and from the clay Pandora was made. She lacked not in beauty, intelligence or grace, the perfect first woman, mother of the human race.

To the brother of Prometheus, Pandora was given, along with a jar from Zeus that shouldn't be opened. But alas her curiosity, a horrible curse, called her to the jar and, not expecting the worst, her fingers did open and from it did fly every ill, every pox, every woe, every lie, every burden of man, every fear, every pain, till all the spirits were gone and only hope remained. Yes, this is a tale of tragedy and woe. Pandora's Jar, our only small hope."

Charis rapidly blinked her eyes to keep herself from crying. When she first helped to write those words, she had had no idea that, a) they would sound so beautiful when spoken by other people, b) they were fact and not fiction, and c) they would, in part, tell her life story. She looked down at Nike, whose expression seemed to say, "Not bad, kid."

The chorus took their places downstage, left.

"Okay, Tyler. We're ready for Zeus." Charis saw Mr. P suppress a smile. She thought she knew why. Tyler was a pudgy kid fighting a losing battle with acne. Charis wondered if Mr. P had cast him as Zeus as some kind of inside joke or to insult the god himself. Tyler leapt as best he could onto the stage.

"Prometheus!" Tyler bellowed from behind his mask. His voice cracked with puberty. "That trickster Titan. He dares defy the Lightning God and give fire to man?"

"Fire! Fire! To the earth from heaven. Man must be stopped lest the gods be forgotten," the chorus chanted.

In anger, Zeus sent a foil-covered, cardboard lightning bolt across the stage. The kids from the prop group gave themselves high-fives. They were pleased with its aerodynamics.

Charis, Gabe, and Nike watched for the remainder of the class as Mr. P directed the play. He moved kids up and downstage, gave lighting cues, and did his best to coax the chorus into actually doing the choreography they'd practiced for weeks.

"What do you think, Nike?" Charis whispered, sinking low in her seat. "Would Zeus approve?"

"Well," she whispered, "Zeus isn't exactly revered for his sense of humor."

Mr. P overheard Nike's whispers with his demigod ears and shot them both a look of disapproval.

"Oops," Nike whispered before becoming still once again. And, just in time too.

"Hey, Charis," Brady said, sitting down in the seat in front of her. He gave a nod to Gabe who gave him one back.

"Hey," she murmured through tight lips. She was afraid the butterflies would flutter from her stomach and out of her mouth. Brady made her so nervous. Not the kind of nervous she felt about dinner tonight, but the "I don't want to say anything stupid because I want you to like me" nervous.

"What do you think?" she asked looking toward the stage. "I think it's going to be great, don't you?"

"Yeah. It's kinda cool seeing everything finally come together." Brady cleared his throat. "Speaking of *together*."

Brady gave Gabe an odd look that caused Gabe to reluctantly excuse himself from Charis's side. He mumbled something about prop malfunctions before walking away.

Brady continued. "I was wondering if we could go to the Jolly Jam dance together? I mean, if you want to go … with me."

"But," Charis said, her face suddenly very hot. "But, I thought you were going with Lauren." The whole school did.

"Nooooo. I didn't know Lauren was going around telling everyone that I invited her to the dance. I didn't." He chuckled. "I mean, she didn't even invite *me*. I don't know what Lauren is thinking most of the time." He shook his head and his dark, impossibly wavy hair moved like it was dancing.

Dancing. The dance. With Brady. Friday. The dance is on Friday.

Charis rolled her eyes and buried her face in her palms causing Brady to think that maybe this wasn't such a good idea after all. He heard through the grapevine that Charis liked him, but maybe it was only gossip. He shifted uncomfortably in his seat.

"Oh, Brady," Charis finally said. "I'd love to go to the dance with you, but I can't." She couldn't believe it. A chance to go to the dance with Brady, and she couldn't take it, she'd be busy taking greater chances with fate. "I already have plans with my family Friday night."

And with destiny too, she wanted to add but didn't. It wasn't fair. *But, fairness doesn't matter, remember?*

"That's okay," he said. "I understand." Brady smiled the melting smile that tilted up on the right side. "Maybe next time?"

"For *sure* next time," she said, careful not to sound too excited.

"Cool. Well, see you around," he said, leaving her there with her mixed emotions.

"Charis and Gabe, come and see me before you head off to your third period classes," Mr. P said. "The rest of you are dismissed. Use these extra few minutes to store your costumes and props properly backstage in the area I showed you earlier. You all have a good afternoon, and I'll see you tomorrow morning. Same place."

The auditorium emptied as kids disappeared behind the stage curtain. Charis grabbed her Nike-equipped backpack and she and Gabe walked toward Mr. P.

"Good work on the writing, guys. You should be proud of yourselves," Mr. P said. "This play would have been worthy of an audience in the *Theatre of Dionysus!*"

Despite his enthusiasm, Charis and Gabe stared blankly at their demigod substitute teacher. They both knew this wasn't what he wanted to talk to them about. Mr. P got the hint.

"So, tonight is the dinner with Alecto," he said. "I'd say don't be afraid, but that's unreasonable, isn't it. So, instead, I'll say be courageous. That *is* within your power. Nike will be there and, with your help, she will keep everything under control, right Nike?" The little goddess glowed gold in response. "You are not under any circumstances to find yourselves alone in the room with Alecto at any time. Understood?"

"Of course! Understood. I wouldn't dream of it," Charis replied.

Mr. P turned his attention to Gabe. "Gabe, since you've elected to get yourself involved in this, I expect you to do your best to protect Charis too. Just keep yourself out of danger in the process."

Gabe promised. In fact, he said "yes sir," which was something Charis had never heard him say before. Not even to her dad.

"It is highly unlikely that Alecto would dare an attack of any sort before any witnesses. That would spell disaster for all of Mt. Olympus and beyond. The goal is always secrecy in these things. I doubt Alecto will do anything to call any unnecessary attention to herself, Hades, or the jar."

Charis's heartbeat quickened as the evening played out in her mind. It made her birthmark ache.

"Do you have any questions?" They didn't. They understood.

"Nike," Mr. P said. "If you need to, and think it's worth the risk of exposure, call to me. For my part, I'll make sure I am alone tonight in case you do." Nike nodded her head in response.

"Okay then," he said, placing his hands on both of their shoulders. "May the Fates smile on all of you." Before Charis could walk away, Mr. P grabbed her chin in his hands. "And, Charis," he said with seriousness in his eyes. "I'll see you tomorrow."

"Count on it, Mr. P."

CHAPTER 22
A LOSS OF APPETITE

THE DINNER IN ALECTO'S HONOR was beautiful. Charis wasn't so nervous that she hadn't noticed. The candles placed throughout the house flickered warm light from the staircase to the front room. White linen, small holiday floral arrangements, and the china and silverware Charis's mom reserved for special occasions decorated the long dining table. In the corner of the family room, a small jazz trio quietly played holiday tunes. A three-person wait staff dressed in crisp black slacks, white shirts, and black bow ties hung around in the kitchen waiting for their silver trays to be filled.

There was a small kitchen crew fussing over a very distinctly Californian menu: crab salad cradled in endive boats, smoked trout and watercress served over granny smith apple slices, shrimp cocktail, pumpkin and lobster bisque, arugula and pear salad, broiled true cod, potato cakes, and grilled asparagus. For dessert? Lemon merengue pie made with lemons from Charis's own backyard. While a Greek menu would have been fine, Charis's mom thought it totally clichéd.

The day's earlier gray clouds became rainy ones. Charis sulked on the couch and looked outside at the wet sheen glossing over everything.

"I believe the words she used when describing this shindig was 'nothing fancy.'" Evan said, kissing Charis on the cheek.

"Hey, Dad," she said, hugging his neck. Her dad usually made her feel so safe. Not tonight. She couldn't imagine he could protect her against Alecto. Her eyes glistened with the tears she wanted to cry. She was going to have to keep it together and not let her emotions get the best of her.

"How was school today?" Evan sat down next to Charis and unlaced his shoes.

"It was good. We had play rehearsal during English. That was *interesting*. Oh, and I took fifth place in the girls' one-mile run today. I think the cool weather helped."

"Way to go, Sunny!" he said, loosening his tie. "By the way, you look lovely tonight." He stood and lifted Charis from the couch, twirling her around.

"Thanks," she said, rolling her eyes. "Mom made me."

"Speaking of ... I'd better go get cleaned up before she *makes* me too, if you know what I mean." The doorbell rang. "Uh oh," Evan said, looking at his watch.

"No, no," Charis said. "It's just, Gabe. He texted me that he was on his way." Charis answered the door.

"Whoa," Gabe said, his eyes big. "You look awesome. Hot even."

"Thanks," she blushed. "You look pretty good yourself. Come on in."

Charis and Gabe did their best to stay out of the way of the hustle and bustle. A cleaned-up Evan and Presley alternated greeting duties once the guests started to arrive. One person at a time, the house came alive with conversation and laughter as the waiters circled the room offering food and wine.

"We can't wait to see the exhibition."

"The ads look great."

"Zeus as a leading man? Brilliant!"

"Have you seen all the press?"

Charis's mom worked the room and made sure everyone had a good time.

"It's about time for the ghoul of honor to arrive, isn't it?" Gabe asked Charis from their corner of the party.

"Yeah," she said looking at him. "I'm a little nervous. Well, more than just a little ... I feel like I could vomit." Charis looked away from Gabe, but he grabbed her face and looked her in the eyes.

"I know. Me too. But, that's okay. We're not supposed to be unafraid. We're supposed to be brave. Right? That's what Mr. P said. Courageous."

Charis told Gabe that Nike felt it best if she stayed upstairs to keep an eye out for any trouble from there. Besides, her mother would have cringed if she had the little goddess attached to her dress tonight.

The doorbell rang and Charis swore she felt its vibrations deep within her birthmark. Her heart sank and her hands got sweaty. Deep inside, Charis knew it was Alecto before she even saw her. Everyone else did too it seemed.

Conversations stalled in mid-sentence and an abrupt silence fell over the room. It was weird. Even the saxophone player bleated out a long, pitchless, mournful note for no reason.

"That must be our guest," Charis's mom said, absently twisting the ring around her finger.

Charis stole a look up the stairs and saw Nike hovering there at the top. It was time.

Mona and Evan opened the door to greet Alecto, or "Mr. Ecto" as she was disguising herself. When Alecto came into view, both of Charis's parents stepped backwards. A small gasp escaped Mona's mouth and Evan grabbed her hand protectively. They stayed that way, speechless and slightly horrified, for a second longer than was comfortable. Richard, Alecto's host from the Getty, was himself standing a considerable distance from her when he cleared his throat and adjusted his tie to break the ice.

"Forgive me," Mona said embarrassed. "Welcome! Welcome to our home." She and Evan motioned them in. "Please come in."

Evan shook Richard's hand and introduced himself. When he moved to do the same with Mr. Ecto, the strange man just stared at his extended hand in disgust. Evan was relieved and not offended at all. He hadn't really wanted to touch him either.

Alecto rather moved into the house than walked into it. Her motion was sloppy and rigid, like these were quite nearly her first steps. Mona guided the new guests into the front room and made introductions.

"Friends, colleagues, and art lovers, please welcome Mr. Richard Burnett, Director for Exhibitions and Public Programs for the Getty Museum, and our distinguished guest and Hellenistic hero of the day, Mr. Al Ecto from Greece."

There was a small round of applause as Richard smiled broadly. Though Alecto attempted a smile herself, to the guests it looked more like a wince. That, of course, caused them all to wince back in response.

Mona grabbed their coats, careful to hold Alecto's as far away as possible because of its strange smell. Charis and Gabe stared in disbelief at the creature masquerading as a human among them. Wasn't it obvious to everyone that there was something seriously wrong with this "Mr. Al Ecto" person? Too tall. Too gray. Too …

"Creep. E," said Gabe. His whole body shook with the willies.

"Charis," her mother called. "Bring Gabe and come meet Mr. Ecto. I'm sure you've lots to talk about with your play and all."

This was it. Charis closed her eyes and said a prayer, *Along with Athena, move also your hand. I am moving, Athena. I hope you are too.*

Charis and Gabe made their way to Alecto. It was an easy path. There were no other guests willing to stand anywhere near her. When Charis finally reached the monster, she saw a fire ignite behind Alecto's eyes.

"Oh," Alecto said through her tiny mouth. "Is thisss your daughter? She's lovely. Lovely, she isss." *Lovely and wicked, wicked, wicked.*

"Charis. Gabe," Mona said. "This is Mr. Ecto, the gentleman who saved the exhibition. Mr. Ecto? Meet my daughter Charis and her best friend Gabe."

If she could get just one word out, Charis knew she'd be okay. Just one.

"Hello. Pleased to meet you, Mr. Ecto." She managed seven.

"Yeah, nice to meet you, Mr. Ecto." Gabe added in a deeper voice than usual.

"Such well-mannered children," Alecto whispered.

The Underworld monster extended her hand toward Charis. Curious, she slowly outstretched her own. It was as she expected. Holding Alecto's hand felt a lot like holding a dead, floppy fish, but worse. It also felt like reliving every nightmare she'd ever had. Charis quickly snatched her hand away before the frightening images could overwhelm her. Amused, Alecto chuckled aloud.

"Yesssss," she muttered. "Very lovely, indeed."

Charis squinted her eyes at her nemesis.

"Mona?" Evan called, distressed. "Can you come here, babe? There's a kitchen question."

Mona excused herself, a little too eagerly as far as Charis was concerned, leaving her and Gabe alone with Alecto. No one could think of much to say, so they just stood there staring at each other.

Charis noticed there was nothing exactly right about Alecto. Her eyes were just a little too small, and were they red? Her nose an eighth of an inch too long, and hooked to the right a bit. And her mouth. That mouth was pinched and small and altogether incapable of a smile. Though her eyes were fixed on Alecto's paper-thin lips, a subtle movement elsewhere caught Charis's attention. Alecto's hair. Charis stared at the deep, black hair on top of Alecto's head. It was so black, it shimmered purple, and so greasy that whole sections of it appeared to lay there stuck together in clumps. Except, it didn't actually *lay* there, it sort of rested.

The snakes!

Just as the chilling fingers of fear began to rise from Charis's heart and clutch her by the throat, her mom returned.

"Well, it looks like it's time to eat. Shall we?"

Alecto mumbled something that Mona did not quite catch.

"Pardon me?" she asked.

"The ressstroom. Where is it?" Alecto asked again.

"Oh, certainly. Follow me, Mr. Ecto" Mona said. "Kids, you go on to the table, okay?"

Alecto clambered into the bathroom and sighed with relief. She was grateful to be away from all those people even if only for a moment. She wasn't accustomed to interacting with them in this way. Before coming to this place, her mission concerning man was simple: punish him, torment him, bring him to justice. But now there was all this conversation and smiling. Alecto looked into the oval mirror and attempted a smile. The snakes on her head hissed and laughed quietly at her painful expression.

"Oh, shut up!" she said, assuming her more natural scowl.

Alecto raised a gray hand and gently blew on her fingers. As she did, her fingernails stretched and grew, razor sharp and dagger like.

"Now ... we ssshall ..."

She carefully picked through the excited snakes on her head as though looking for ripe fruit to pluck.

"Ah. Basanizo!" she said with affection. She raised a shiny black snake above the others. It wrapped itself tightly around her finger, flicking its tongue in and out.

"My ssspecial pet. My tormenting little angel. Thisss will hurt a bit."

Using her pointy fingernail, Alecto sliced back and forth through the thick, fleshy bottom of the serpent. Before long, she pulled the writhing and moaning snake away from her bleeding head. The pain from her self-inflicted wound quickened her own breathing and red-stained tears streaked down her face.

"Yesss, my dear, it hurtsss a bit, but it is worth the injury you will inflict upon the girl. Upon the girl, you will inflict a great injury, my Basanizo."

The snake thrashed left and right in her hand until it at last stopped bleeding.

"There, there."

Alecto bent down low to the floor.

"Go to her bedroom. Go. Wait with great patience. Wait. Then, when the time is right, ssstrike to kill. Kill!"

Basanizo slowly slithered out of her palm and slid beneath the bathroom door. Like a ghost, the snake wound his way through numerous pairs of shoes, narrowly escaping a heel or two, and climbed the stairs.

In the bathroom, Alecto wiped her blood-streaked face and quieted her hair down. Her task here was nearly done. She would be reunited with her sisters soon.

"Oh," she said giggling, reaching for the doorknob. "Mustn't do that."

She blew on her hand once more and her dagger-like fingernails disappeared in a puff of smoke.

"Now, to enjoy someone's last sssupper."

CHAPTER 23
A SIDE OF BLOOD AND GORE

CHARIS WAS RELIEVED to discover nameplates when she got to the table. She and Gabe would be sitting across from Alecto. *Good,* she thought. *This way I can keep an eye on her.* She impressed herself with her new militaristic thinking. Hanging out with the Goddess of Victory apparently had its benefits. Feeling capable was one of them.

Charis watched Alecto as the creature ate, disgusted. For such a small mouth, she kept it overstuffed with second and third helpings of every dish. Alecto didn't say much, but maybe that was because her mouth was full. She was an eating machine. However, the two people sitting on either side of her, Richard and another unfortunate representative from the museum, hardly ate at all. Surely, the sights, sounds, and smells of the greedy guest between them had ruined their appetites.

* * *

Basanizo the snake finally slithered his way into Charis's room. He raised his hooded head and scanned his surroundings for the best place to hide. He decided that Charis's lace bed skirts were perfect. As the child climbed into bed, he would grab her ankles fast with his fangs and generously pump his deadly venom. The glands in his mouth stung with poison at the thought of piercing Charis's skin.

Basanizo flicked his black tongue and chuckled. The carpet warmed his underbelly as he slid across the room. It felt good. He had spent his whole his life on top of Alecto's head living in a nest with a bunch of other snakes. But this, *this* was what being a snake should feel like.

*   *   *

When dessert was served, Mona asked Charis and Gabe to share their play with Alecto. The other dinner guests applauded, coaxing them on. The two friends reluctantly stood and Charis rolled her eyes, annoyed.

"May as well get this over with, huh?" Charis said, looking directly at her mother. Mona responded with a frown, surprised at her daughter's snark.

"Well, the play is called *World of Woe: The Story of Pandora, a Jar, and the 5 o'clock News.*" There were murmurs of approval from around the table. "It's a modern day take on the myth of Pandora's Jar."

At this Alecto sat straight up, stopped her incessant shoveling of food, and stared the girl in the eye. A minuscule but devilish grin found her lips.

"The play, of course, begins with the chorus. Historic documents tell us that most tragic plays started that way, so …"

Alecto leaned forward, staring more closely at Charis. In spite of all the food she had just eaten, Charis thought she had a hungry look on her face. Gabe saw it too and bravely stepped closer to his friend, all the while rubbing his head.

"After the chorus," Charis continued, "Zeus comes to the stage and explains why he created Pandora in the first place."

The mention of Zeus's name broke Alecto from her stare. She bowed her head briefly, as if in reverence.

"The story of Pandora and her jar begins with the Titan, Prometheus. One day Zeus told Prometheus to make man from water and the earth, so he did. Over time, Prometheus grew to like man more than the gods. Because of that, he started giving man gifts and teaching man skills to make him more powerful. Zeus didn't especially like that. Prometheus did other things to make Zeus mad, but the main thing he did was steal fire from Mt. Olympus and give it to man. That was more than Zeus could take, and Zeus wanted revenge ... on everyone."

*   *   *

From the moment Alecto excused herself to the bathroom Nike was on guard. Standing knee-deep in carpet behind the opened bedroom door, she heard Basanizo slink his way up the stairs. The fire that always burned through Nike's veins before a battle ignited within her. She glowed a sterling silver just like the sword in her hand. Nike raised her legs high through the carpet and quietly inched herself to the very end of the door to peek around it. She watched as Basanizo twisted his way into the room. From the floor, the snake was almost as tall as Nike. Its shiny scales were like a wall slithering by. Nike knew she must be careful. She must have wisdom. She must kill or else be killed.

*   *   *

At the dinner table, Charis continued.

"To avenge the theft, Zeus told Hephaestus ... he was like the god of technology, fire, and crafts and stuff ... to make a woman—the *first* human woman. Zeus told the other gods to give this woman gifts. The gods, lots of them, gave her many different treasures, and she was blessed with lots of great, great things. You know, she was intelligent and eloquent. She was beautiful. She was rich. Anyway, because she was so blessed by the gods, Hermes named her Pandora. That means 'all gifted' ..."

By now, Alecto was clutching the white linen tablecloth in her hands.

Pandora! Every ill on earth could be traced back to that one.

How Alecto would have loved to torment her!

* * *

As Basanizo continued to enjoy his belly rub from the carpet upstairs, Nike shot up to the bed's surface, careful not to make a sound. From overhead, she watched him move closer to a position beneath the bed. She couldn't let that happen. It would be easier to strike him out in the open before he slithered into a more confined space. Nike wanted to keep the advantage of flight, something hard to do under a bed.

* * *

Charis had the dinner guests in the palm of her hand as she continued her story. "Zeus had Pandora made as a gift to Prometheus's brother, Epimetheus." Charis stopped to laugh. She couldn't help it.

"Wait. Can you believe it? Giving a *person* as a wedding gift? As the bride?" There was giggling around the table.

"Ridiculous ..."

"Whoa. Whoooaaaa," Gabe said, finally realizing he wasn't mute. "I don't know about you, but I could think of a *few* ladies I wouldn't mind Zeus handing over to me!"

The table erupted in laughter.

* * *

The burst of noise from downstairs caused Basanizo to stop his slithering. He raised his wide head and listened for signs of trouble. While he didn't *hear* any, he did *see* one, above. Looking up from the carpet, he saw a small bolt of lightning just before it rained down on his head. His halted movement was exactly the opportunity Nike had hoped for.

*   *   *

"May I continue … *Gabe?*" Charis asked when the laughter subsided.

"When Pandora was presented to her husband, she came with another gift from Zeus as well. It was a jar. Prometheus had warned his brother Epimetheus not to accept any gifts from Zeus. Prometheus was afraid they could be nothing more than tricks or something, and he was right. Epimetheus didn't listen though, and he took both Pandora and the jar for himself."

Before she went on with her story, Charis couldn't help but add her own disclaimer.

"In Pandora's defense, she really didn't know what was in the jar. Nor did she know she shouldn't open it, so …"

*   *   *

Upstairs, in the heat of battle, Nike missed her first blow. The snake looked up and saw her descending toward him at the last moment. Within that split second, Basanizo recoiled his black head and avoided the goddess's strike. As Nike turned back toward the sky, the snake struck her with his deadly fangs. Had she not positioned her shield against the blow, it could have been a fatal one.

Looking up at the little warrior above him, the snake sensed his disadvantage. Basanizo made a getaway for the bed. Beneath *it* was a more level playing field. Nike had to stop him, so she flung her sword toward the creature's back. It sliced through the air and landed true to the mark, severing Basanizo's spine. The muscles in the snake's body quaked, trying to expel the weapon.

*   *   *

At the dinner table, Alecto squirmed in her seat, wincing as Charis continued to speak.

"… before I finish this, there is something I want to say."

There was a new seriousness to Charis's presentation.

"I love the story of Pandora. But, I hate it too."

Charis looked to Gabe for encouragement and he nodded his head, urging her on.

"When the gods gave Pandora her gifts, curiosity was included with all of the rest of them. And, it was curiosity that led her to open Zeus's booby-trapped jar. She didn't know that inside the jar were all these bad things or evil spirits. Nor did she know that by opening it she would release such an awful plague on the world. But, she did open the jar, and that's exactly what happened."

Charis thought about how often her own questions led her into trouble. But her questions also compelled her want to figure things out, get good grades, make friends, or discover new things.

"I hate that curiosity is to blame for mankind's trouble. It just doesn't make sense to me. It makes it seem like we would be better off remaining ignorant or something. I don't get that." The ringlet of hair that she'd been toying with from the start was now wound tightly around her finger.

"And, I hate that it was the gods who set the whole thing up. I mean, how unfair is that? They gave her the curiosity that was ultimately her punishment. *Our* punishment. What kind of gods are they anyway?"

She thought about Athena and Nike and how much she had grown to love them, and yet, they were a part of the Pandora problem too. They were guilty too. It was all so complicated, this god thing. Charis didn't feel any wiser about them now than she did before, even after meeting a few face-to-face. Tears reached for her eyes for the second time that night.

* * *

Nike swooped down to the wounded snake and delivered a blow to his head with her shield. Basanizo's head crashed to the ground and he hissed in pain. At the same time downstairs, Alecto squeezed her eyes shut and brought her fingers to her temples, massaging them.

*   *   *

Charis breathed through her urge to cry, partly because she didn't want to embarrass herself and partly because she didn't want Alecto to think she was afraid.

"And, Zeus did all of this because he felt man would be too powerful with fire. So, what? Did he think that man wouldn't need the gods anymore if they had fire? Did he think that the only way man would continue to revere the gods was through ignorance and fear, or if he was kept in the dark? Was Zeus afraid that love alone wasn't reason enough for man to continue to worship?"

*   *   *

Before Nike could deliver her fatal blow, Basanizo wiggled free of her sword and sent it flying out of his back and into the air. The airborne sword distracted Nike and gave the snake an opportunity to hurl his grand head into her. It landed squarely on her armored chest. The impact shot Nike into a wall and her little silver light started to dim.

*   *   *

"That's why I hate the story," Charis said, solemnly. "But, I love it too. I love it because it doesn't end all hopeless and awful. Yes, evil escaped into the world and still exists right now." Charis bit her lip, thinking.

"You know, as we wrote our play, Mr. P, I mean, Mr. *Papadakis,* told us to find evidence of Pandora's evil spirits in the world today. That was probably the easiest homework I've had all year."

A titter of nervous laughter broke Charis's heaviness.

"It's kinda sad but true … nothing like reading gossip blogs to bring a tragic myth to real life!"

Everyone giggled but Alecto. She sat there with her face pinched, looking nauseated and nervous. Her skin glistened with sweat and was even grayer than when she first arrived.

* * *

Basanizo's big head hovered high above the crumpled Nike beneath him. A devious pleasure played upon his scaly face. This was going to be good. In one swift movement, he drew his head back and lunged for Nike, fangs bared.

* * *

"But, like I said, the story of Pandora is not all bad news. There is still one spirit that remains in the jar. Her name is Elpis; it means 'Hope'," Charis said, wistfully.

"And Hope ..."

"Should remain there," said Alecto, in her loudest voice all night.

The pounding in her head from Basanizo's battle upstairs made everything fuzzy, loud, and too much.

"There hope should remain. Do you not agree? Girl? The disaster that would result if Hope were to essscape would be catastrophic. No?"

"I, I don't know. I don't think it ..."

Wicked, wicked girl.

Alecto rose from her chair, startling everyone by this, her most vigorous display of the evening. She leaned forward against the table and, even from across them, towered over both Charis and Gabe.

"I'm telling you. There, in Pandora's Jar, Hope should remain."

Her words were clipped. Pinched. Her eyes, red. Focused.

Charis swallowed. Hard. She was ready to accept whatever followed. Maybe Mr. P was wrong. Maybe Alecto would strike her here, in front of everyone. Charis would do her best to survive it. The girl knew she had a job to do and she hadn't done it yet. Charis Parks wouldn't go down without a fight.

"I disagree," she said, firmly, sticking her chest out and throwing her shoulders back.

"I think Hope should be released, and," she paused, hoping Alecto could read into the code of her next words, "I happen to know I'm not the only one who thinks so."

*   *   *

As Basanizo closed in on Nike, his mouth watering in anticipation, the little goddess jumped to her feet. Determined, she shot toward the beast's open mouth, grimacing and baring her own teeth. When Nike reached his poisonous fangs, she grabbed one in each hand. A look of horrible surprise seized the unfortunate snake's eyes as he felt the bones start to crack inside his face.

In her grip of steel and might, Nike held on to Basanizo's fangs and flew headlong into his opened mouth. With every beat of her tiny wings, she plunged deeper and deeper into his long, scaly body. Squirming with all of her strength, Nike flew past the living warmth of his heart and lungs, stomach and guts. Bones, muscle, blood, and tissue broke, splintered, and turned in on themselves. Fueled with the strength of every battle she'd ever fought, Nike pushed her way through the creature's gyrating body with his black scales trailing behind.

Nike punctured Basanizo's flesh using his own fangs like daggers and burst through the other end of his bloodied corpse. When she emerged, the snake was nothing more than a lifeless heap turned a gruesome inside-out on the floor.

A war cry. She wanted a long, loud war cry. But, in this realm, on the earth and in disguise, that was not possible. So, Nike shined in brilliant light instead. In a rainbow of spectacular colors, her light exploded across the walls of Charis's room. A miraculous spectacle.

*   *   *

As Alecto argued with the little girl, a wave of blackness crashed over her. The creature rocked unsteadily back and forth before rolling her eyes back and falling to the floor. She brought the tablecloth and all of its contents down with her in her clinched, clammy hands.

"Oh, God!" Mona cried. "Someone get water. Get a cold towel."

Overcoming great reluctance, Mona leaned over Alecto and wiped her brow until the monster posing as a curator's eyes fluttered open.

"Are you okay, Mr. Ecto?" Mona asked.

Alecto was horrified.

"Get me out of here. At once!" she yelled with her little mouth. "Now!"

"Of course," Richard answered. "Of course."

"Charis, go get Mr. Burnett's and Mr. Ecto's things, honey," Mona said, calmly.

Richard and Alecto were at the door when Charis returned with their belongings. Alecto still appeared weak, dizzy, pained. No matter. Charis stood defiantly before her enemy as she handed her the coat. There were awkward exchanges and goodbyes as Mona opened the door to the evening air and showed her guests out. Before long, Richard and Alecto disappeared into the wet, December night.

What happened? Basanizo. Basanizo. What happened to my beloved?

Alecto's head throbbed and ached. So did her heart.

As the Erinyes Sister looked back toward the house, hostility overflowing within her black heart, she was rather startled by what she saw. Squinting her beady eyes, Alecto spied a little light in Charis's bedroom window; a light with a ferocious face, a drawn sword, and Basanizo's head clutched in one outstretched hand.

What? What? That could only be ... Nike! How?

As the onslaught of confusion threatened Alecto's already flimsy composure, she watched in disbelief as Charis and Gabe took their places beside the little goddess. The three of them looked down upon her from the bedroom, unflinching and unremorseful. Once more, unable to stop the wave of impending darkness, Alecto's mouth kissed the ground as she fainted away on the concrete.

THURSDAY

There must always remain something that is antagonistic to good.

—PLATO

CHAPTER 24
NOTHING SIMPLE ABOUT IT

In spite of all the excitement last night—a menacing guest, an assassination attempt, and the death of one ugly snake in her bedroom—Charis slept like a rock. There was no visit from Athena—at least, none that she could remember. Just long, deep, peaceful, sound sleep. She would have slept longer were it not for her alarm.

Charis sat up in bed and looked for Nike. The little goddess was sitting in the window, still keeping guard.

"Morning, Nike," Charis said in a yawn.

"Good morning," Nike responded without turning her head. "I trust you slept well?"

"Like a baby." Charis answered. She joined Nike at the window and looked out at the day. No more clouds, just the beginnings of sunshine. The two looked quite a pair, Charis in her pink heart flannel pajamas and Nike still clad in the armor of last night.

"Anything else happen last night?"

"No. Nothing." Nike stood up and placed her tiny hands on her tiny hips.

"Charis, I'm troubled. After sitting up all night thinking about it, I still don't know why Alecto would attempt your assassination. That's not like her. Something or someone has put her up to this." She shrugged her shoulders. "It's puzzling. I want to discover why."

"'Why' would be good to know," Charis agreed. "It always is." She found some comfort knowing the gods themselves had questions every now and again.

"I need to speak with Hermes and Athena. Today. Something is troubling me about all of this," Nike continued.

"You can do that? From here?" Charis hoped so. The idea of Nike flitting off somewhere far away to go talk to the gods with Alecto and her snakes still out there wasn't Charis's idea of protection.

"Yes. It's like Erichthonius, I mean, *Mr. P*, said," Nike explained. "I just need to turn my concentrated energy and thoughts to them and we're brought into one another's presence. There is a risk however … thus our reluctance. When gods within this realm communicate with other gods, it compromises our disguises and humans can see us more fully. The results are often disastrous, murderous even."

Nike chuckled.

"*Or* they're comical, and make front-page news in tabloid magazines. You know … 'Alien Sighting in Garland, Nebraska' kind of thing."

Charis twirled a lock of hair around her finger, thinking.

"So, you need to be alone today. You can't go with me to school."

"That's right."

After a few seconds, her eyes brightened with an idea.

"But, I want to see Athena too, and I want to meet Hermes … bearing his 'mark' and everything."

Nike had figured as much. She knew Charis wouldn't want to miss this opportunity.

"Do you think I could stay here, with you?"

"Do as you please, Charis," Nike answered.

Charis took her shower. She had to make it look like she was at least *trying* to go to school. She would go downstairs and say she was sick. No … no, that would mean one of her parents would stay home with her. She would say she was still tired from last night.

Yes. That's it.

The family had talked for hours after their guests left. They sat around the table and replayed the events surrounding the outrageous Mr. Ecto and his strange behavior. Charis mostly listened, afraid she couldn't trust her own words and that she'd reveal more than she should. What a night it had been.

I'll say I'm too tired. That should work.

She paused.

That should work?

As she stepped out of the shower, it dawned on Charis what she was about to do. She was about to lie to her parents. What's worse, she felt like she didn't have much choice in the matter.

She had an obligation to herself and to the gods to figure this jar thing out. Even if she had the time to, she didn't think she could explain any of this to her parents without them thinking she'd gone crazy. There was no other way. She wanted to speak with Athena and Hermes. She hated that she had to lie to do it. Why did it have to be so complicated? Why weren't things black and white?

Before the fog disappeared from the mirror, Charis quickly wrote lyrics to a favorite Taylor Swift song, *Never Grow Up*: " … it could still be simple."

Charis had done a lot of growing up in the past few days. And no, there was nothing simple about it.

She dressed in fresh pajamas and went downstairs. Her family was already in the kitchen continuing last night's conversation.

"When that dude fell down, I couldn't believe it," Presley was saying.

"I just figured he'd gotten himself all worked up in his debate with Sunny, which went too far, by the way. 'There hope ssshould remain!' That was one ssstrange man."

"Hey guys," Charis said.

"Hey, sweetheart," Mona responded. She looked at her daughter, who was standing there with wet hair and in her pj's.

"You okay?"

Charis took a deep breath and dove headfirst into her lie.

"I, I guess so. But, I'm really tired. It took me forever to fall asleep last night with all the excitement. That Mr. Ecto person kind of freaked me out. I didn't mean to upset him."

She looked at the sympathy on each of their faces and knew they were buying it.

"If I email my teachers for my assignments, can I stay home today? And, before you say no, you know I don't do this. Ever."

Mona and Evan agreed.

"Make sure the doors are locked and the alarm is on. Keep your cellphone on you at all times," her dad said.

Evan went through the safety checklist. If only he knew that Charis couldn't be any safer than she was right now with the Goddess of Victory upstairs in her bedroom.

"And get some rest, baby girl," Evan said. "My last meeting is at one o'clock. I'll come home immediately after, okay?"

Charis hugged her dad's neck.

"Thanks, you guys," Charis sighed.

"Wait, I'm tired too," Presley insisted.

"Not a chance," said Mona.

Charis was able to stay home with Nike. She'd be able to see Athena, and finally meet Hermes. As she looked at the parents she just deceived to make this possible, Charis felt good and horrible about it.

CHAPTER 25
ALECTO CALLS FOR HELP

DURING THE NIGHT, the front desk clerk at the W Hotel received three calls, each one complaining about the noises coming from Room 1206. Every time he went up to look into it, he was met with silence, or once, a demand that he just go away … *or else.*

For her part, Alecto passed the night mourning, in pain, and seething in anger. Her head hurt. It was bad enough when she cut Basanizo from her scalp, but then to lose him to death was more than she could bear. The wound throbbed with phantom pain, as if the snake still rested there, fatally injured. She sobbed anew thinking about it. She was, for all intents and purposes, an immortal creature, and wholly unaccustomed to personal loss and death. Basanizo was a part of her. She shuddered wondering about the violence of his last moments. Alecto didn't have to guess about the excruciating pain he had felt *during* them. She had felt it for herself, connected as they are … they were. Nike, most certainly, brutalized him. The goddess's reputation for victory, at all cost and in every way, was the stuff of legends among the legends.

Alecto rubbed the sticky place where Basanizo once lived and heaved again. The other snakes upon her head were sad, limp, and listless too. As much as Alecto missed her beloved Basanizo, his death wasn't the only reason for her tears. She had failed. She had failed in her mission to extinguish the child, the Grace.

Nike!

In hindsight, she should have known others might be privy to their little mission. It's hard to keep things, even secret things, from the gods. That, and Hades wasn't exactly known for his ability to keep secrets. His arrogance didn't see the need. He'd probably bragged about his intentions, unafraid that anyone would dare do anything about it.

However it happened that Alecto was discovered, letting Hades down was what she had been most afraid of. Deep within the bleak caverns of the Underworld, Alecto had witnessed his wrath countless times and it was nothing pretty. There was no telling what he would do to her or her sisters. He would, no doubt, be merciless.

Hadesss.

Alecto's little, thin lip curled at the thought of him. She was surprised to find herself angry with the dark god, and that frightened her. Hades should be revered. He should be respected, but she didn't feel like it right now. He was responsible for her present predicament, mourning on the floor of a hotel room. About her predicament ... something just didn't seem right.

The girl, precocious as she was, didn't seem *evil*. Opinionated, yes. Strong-willed, yes. But evil? In her line of work Alecto saw her fair share of evil. All of the people she ever tormented deserved it. Murderers. Thieves. The lot of them. She was happy to dispense with the justice they had coming. But this girl, this *Charis* ... Alecto wasn't sure.

Even with her questions, Alecto realized she had no reason to doubt Hades. He was so upset and concerned that the jar might fall into the wrong hands. He was convinced that, should it, it would be the end of mankind. He could hardly keep from exploding in rage talking about it. She hadn't known he had such affection for man, but Hades was often misunderstood.

Alecto had long believed that Hades had an undeserved reputation. She could understand how though. He was Lord of the Underworld, King of the Dead. He was a little frightening to man. But, in reality, he performed his duties fairly, without malice and in good judgment.

Pah! People often fear the unknown, and death most certainly is that. But what about the girl?

All of this thinking about Basanizo, Hades, and the girl caused Alecto to breathe another whimper.

She rose from the bed she'd made on the floor, the hotel mattress too soft for her to sleep on, and opened the heavy curtains. The light from the sun made her wince. Her beady eyes, already small, were nearly swollen shut from crying.

"Nike!" she hissed aloud, thinking of the evening again.

Who else knew? Why was Nike there? And, the child ... the child, she knew who I was all along.

Then, like a breaking dawn, it occurred to Alecto that she could be in the middle of a most terrible war. Hades. Hades was trying to save mankind and the girl, the girl and Nike and ... who knows who else ... were trying to, what? Destroy it? Had the gods finally tired of man and his self-destructive behavior? His arrogance? His godlessness? Were they attempting to extinguish him? Was the girl, this calculating girl, working to aid them?

This is bad. This is very, very bad.

Alecto's heart raced. She drew the curtains closed and allowed the returning dark to comfort her. She bowed on knobby knees and pressed her forehead to the ground. With her eyes closed, she began to whisper.

"Sssisters. Sssisters. Sssisters."

Sweat formed on her brow.

"Sssisters. Sssisters. Sssisters."

Her face, whether from pain or concentration, began to twist and contort. Her human facade dissolved like wax on a candle.

"Sssisters. Sssisters. Sssisters."

Her face, her true face, slowly emerged and the wings on her back unfolded and rose high above her. Alecto flung her face to the sky. Her eyes glazed over, in a trance.

Somewhere in the gray void, in a timeless, spaceless place between the Underworld and Gaia, the earth, the Erinyes Sisters met. The three sisters stood in silence. They were not to contact one another except in dire circumstances or certain danger.

"Alecto, why have you called us here, sister?" Megaera asked. "Danger?"

'Danger' rose from her smoky face and formed a white halo circling all three of them.

"Quite possibly, we all are in danger," said Alecto, her soundless mouth moving. It was good to speak with her sisters here. She did not need to use her voice, which had grown so tired from speaking with the humans.

"We all, posssibly ..."

Tisiphone looked at Alecto intently, like a bird upon her prey.

"Meaning, dear Alecto. What do you mean?"

"The girl," she answered.

"What of ... 'the girl'?" spat Tisiphone in fire.

"To the girl's house I went. At the proper time, I did let my Basanizo go."

Alecto fought hard against the tears that threatened. She didn't want to appear weak before her sisters.

"Basanizo did go to the girl's room to ssstrike her. To ssstrike her, he went as I instructed."

The snakes surrounding the place where Basanizo once lived parted, exposing the shallow, red wound. His only remnant.

"Ssslaughtered," the snakes hissed. "Ssslaughtered!"

Megaera gasped, her smoky face nearly disappeared within her inhale.

"Your beloved," she shrieked.

"How?" Tisiphone demanded. "How did he meet his end?"

Alecto drew nearer to her sisters, folding her wings around them.

"Nike. Nike the Warrior Goddess. Nike the Winged Victory. Nike!"

Aghast! They couldn't believe it!

What was she doing on Gaia? How did she know Alecto was there? Was she sure it was Nike? What did it mean? Surely, if Nike was there then Athena, Athena must also be a conspirator! She always did think she knew what was best for man. Pah! "Goddess of Wisdom.". And, the child? Did the girl child know? She did? Heartless! Vile! To speak so freely of releasing the last hope for her own kind! Monster! Monster!

"There is a conspiracy for the fall of man," Alecto assured. "A conssspiracy among the gods for mankind's fall, and the girl, the evil girl helpsss them. That is why Hades wishes to stop the girl. Hades alone stands against the other gods and this girl. That is why we must ..."

"We must tell Hades!" shouted Tisiphone.

"No!" cried Alecto. "No. We mustn't do that. But we must listen for any discord among the gods. Spy for any plot. Give me time. I need time."

Megaera shook her head no.

"Help. You need help, not time." She understood what it was to be alone in your own failure, your own shame. The memory of hers that night at the museum was still tender.

"Yes, help," said Tisiphone. Alecto's pride hated to admit it, but with Nike involved she alone was no match.

"We shall come to you ..."

"In sssecret!" Alecto insisted.

"In secret," they agreed.

It was risky, and they wouldn't have much time. Hades would certainly notice their absence. The number of new souls into his kingdom would decline minus their impressive contribution. Hades was obsessed about that. But, if they were not gone too long, perhaps it was possible. Besides, Hades hadn't been his usual vigilant self, preoccupied as he was with the jar. In fact, Tisiphone realized that she had not seen the god lately. Hades had gone missing. Still, they must use caution. Another failure in his eyes could mean their end. They had few friends in the spirit realm; they needn't make any more enemies ... especially none the likes of Hades.

"The jar," Tisiphone said. "We will get the jar." They all nodded their snake-filled heads.

Pointing a bony finger to her oozing scalp, still aching from its recent loss, Alecto added, "and the girl ... we will get that damned girl."

CHAPTER 26
A GODLY GET-TOGETHER

CHARIS: Hey. Staying home today. Cn u tell mr. p abt last night?

      Gabe: Yep. U cool?

Charis: Yeah. Don't worry. News to talk to some peeps.

Charis: Need, not news. : /

      Gabe: As in her peeps?

Charis: Yeah. I'll ttyl about it.

      Gabe: K.

      Gabe: This is cray right?

Charis: Very.

Charis went back to her room to "sleep." When she finally heard her brother leave, she jumped from her bed and walked through the house to make sure everyone was gone.

"Okay," she said to Nike. "What do we do now?"

"*We* don't do anything." Nike flew from the nightstand to the ground where she knelt to her knees. "You'd better hop on your bed, just in case."

Charis didn't know what the "just in case" was for but she hopped on her bed anyway. Nike pressed her head to the floor and was nearly buried within the threads of carpet. Charis peeked over the edge of her bed and looked down at Nike. She was so tiny. Tiny and mighty.

"Athena. Hermes. Come," she whispered.

Her body pulsated a white light. She had a glowing ring all around her.

"Athena. Hermes. Come."

The light reached farther and farther up and out finally reaching Charis up on her bed. She scooted back, unsure.

"Athena. Hermes. Come."

Nike threw her head back and disappeared in the blast of radiant color that followed. The impact shoved Charis against the headboard. She covered her eyes against the bright light. The room was quiet, really quiet. The way quiet feels submerged beneath water.

Charis peeled her hands from her eyes and opened them when she thought it was safe. She couldn't believe what she saw. She was no longer in her bedroom, not really. But, she didn't know where she was, or if it was a place at all. It was more like she was in a feeling. A feeling of nothingness and everything. Stillness and motion. Beginning and end. A feeling that everything that has ever been anything has always made perfect sense.

It didn't take long for Charis to realize she wasn't alone. Nike was there in the feeling too. But, Charis had never seen Nike like this before. She was tall. Taller than any other woman Charis had ever met. Raven-colored hair hung to her waist. Her legs looked like they were made of clay and sculpted by the hands of a master. Her wings glowed and shimmered like two stars. And her eyes sparkled a sincere emerald, rich and lush and full of all things green. Charis would have been sorely afraid had she not felt such love. Love and awe.

"Charis," Nike said in a voice much bigger than before. She motioned for Charis to look ahead, forward. There she saw them, in the mist of the moment. Athena was there, and as beautiful as she was in her dream. The goddess was her very own sun.

And that had to be Hermes. He wore his wavy, silver hair like a crown. His face was handsome, but Charis could tell it could also be severe. Like the others, he was perfectly made, strong, sure, and able. And, though he stood almost naked and wrapped in a stingy bit of cloth, Charis didn't feel embarrassed. His nakedness was honest and pure, there was nothing shameful about it.

Hermes walked toward her. No, that's not right. He glided. Before he even spoke a word, Charis felt wrapped in a blanket of affection and nearly burst into tears, overjoyed by it.

"Charis." The Messenger God said her name like a prayer. It was ice cream and laughter.

"I've … *we've* looked for you for such a long time."

The words Hermes spoke were true. Charis cupped her hands to her heart. She was so happy to be found.

"What a delight it is to finally meet you, my image bearer," Hermes continued.

Charis's birthmark came to life, but it didn't itch or ache this time. This time it warmed her, from the inside out.

Athena walked up to join them. She placed a hand on Charis's shoulder.

"Are you okay? I didn't want to disturb your rest last night. I thought after such an eventful evening, sleep was the best thing."

"I'm fine," Charis said, smiling, belonging.

"Then, Nike," Athena said looking at the Warrior Goddess, "what brings the two of you here?"

"Something is not right, Athena," Nike answered.

It was not news that Hades had the jar. Hermes was the one to discover it and retrieve it from him. Further, the alliance between Hades and the Erinyes Sisters was well-known and solid. They worked in harmony together, keeping the balance of the Underworld and Gaia. However, Alecto's willingness to punish an innocent like Charis was an affront the likes of which Nike had never seen.

"You should have heard that monster arguing with Charis about the importance of keeping Elpis in Pandora's Jar. It makes no sense. Alecto is absolutely convinced it is the right thing. Convinced to the point of attempting murder to ensure it. The murder of an innocent! Why would she do that? Why would she break the code of conduct that has governed her and her sisters since the beginning?" Nike's eyes were black, just like the words she spoke.

"There is more to this story than we know." Nike hesitated. "I don't believe Alecto is acting on her own. It pains me to say it, but I think Hades has put her up to this. This is no longer merely about theft. It is far worse than that. I suspect he's up to something, something that might have grave consequences for all of our worlds."

Nike felt remorse about even suspecting ill motives of Hades. He was a god who deserved her admiration like every other. But they had to be sure.

Hermes spoke, slowly and with caution. He understood the delicacy with which such charges must be handled.

"Hades does not suspect that it was I who took the jar," he said. Charis rode the smooth river of his words.

"I have been before him daily and have no reason to think otherwise. I will continue my duties in the Underworld and keep a keen eye out for anything unusual."

"Yes," said Athena. "Yes. And Nike, my wisdom says that Alecto will be undeterred in her attempts against our Charis. She will come back stronger, and possibly with her sisters. You must be prepared in such an event."

That sent chills down Charis's spine. Athena sensed this and leaned down close to her face.

"But you mustn't worry. All will be well. We'll see to it."

"Is there anything I can do?" Charis asked. She hated feeling like everyone was doing everything for her while she herself did nothing.

"Yes, Charis," Hermes said, embracing her with his words. "You can be true to your destiny. You can be unwavering in the face of the obstacles ahead. That's all any of us can do."

"Sunny?" The voice sounded a million gajillion miles away. "You awake?"

"Oh my God ... Gods!" Charis stammered. "My dad is home."

The feeling they were in began to fade and float away. The real world of birthdays, swim meets, and head colds started rushing back.

"Trust in yourself and in us, Charis," Athena called. "That's the best you can ever do."

In a final wind, Charis was back in her room on her bed. Nike lay on the floor, a keychain.

"Sunny?"

"Up here, dad." He walked into her room and she forced a yawn.

"Wow!" he smiled. "You've been asleep a long time, kiddo." Charis looked at the clock. It read 2:12. Time worked tricky in nowhere.

*   *   *

Athena and Hermes returned to Hermes's temple at Mt. Olympus.

"She's brave, that one," Hermes said. "'Is there anything I can do?' She has a lion's heart."

"She does," Athena agreed. "I know her bravery will be put to the test, but I believe she will withstand it. She must, or there is no hope."

Hermes grabbed Athena's hand. "Hope is alive and well, sister. And the hands of Grace will release her into the world. You will see." His honey-coated words were sweet to Athena's ears. "Now dear sister, I must return to the Underworld. There are souls who need guidance and a Hades who needs monitoring."

Hermes kissed Athena on her cheek and flew from the shining mountain with lightning speed. Athena walked toward her temple, deep in contemplation and prayer.

In the golden, deserted temple of Hermes, from out of the thin air, a dark shadow appeared. It was Hades. He held his Helm of Darkness gripped in his hands.

So, it was Hermes who stole Pandora's Jar.

He might have known. He looked up with disgust at the naked alabaster statue of Hermes looming arrogantly above him.

And now Athena and Nike are involved too, are they?

Hades clinched his jaw against the fear and anger threatening to overtake him.

Since Alecto had failed, it was up to him to get Charis. He would get to the girl and bring her to the Underworld.

For safekeeping ...

CHAPTER 27
IT'S JUST A JAR, RIGHT?

RICHARD TRIED TO REACH 'Mr. Al Ecto' all morning.

"This is ridiculous," he mumbled to himself, dialing Alecto's room again. "Some help he's been … nothing but trouble. Strange, weird, trouble."

Richard paced in the hotel lobby listening to the bad mix of dance music through the overhead speakers. He was going to give it ten more minutes and then he would bolt. Any longer, and he'd prepare for the gallery talk himself. That's probably what he should have done in the first place, but he knew that that would not have pleased the exhibition's investors. Both corporate and individual sponsors not only gave generously to the show itself, but also to get Mr. Ecto here to replace that screw-up Mr. Ward.

Richard sat down on the purple leather couches in the waiting area. He stared off into space, replaying the events of last night's dinner party in his head. He thought the whole thing, while beautiful and well-intentioned (he'd come to expect no less from Mona), was simply a disaster.

Why was Mr. Ecto so aggressive with Mona's kid? What's her name? Charis.

He was surprised that Mona hadn't told him off. But the truth was, she didn't really have time to because before anyone could say anything, **BOOM**! Down goes Mr. Ecto. Richard laughed out loud in spite of himself and then looked around to see if anyone noticed.

Man, the look on that guy's face when he came to.

Richard shook his baldhead side to side. Mr. Ecto was a strange man. After last night, Richard realized he wasn't the only person to think so. He looked down at his phone.

Three more minutes. That's it.

He crossed his legs and impatiently tapped his foot to the rhythm of the bad music. Just then, the elevators opened and out stalked Alecto. Richard pounced to his feet and forced a smile on his rather serious looking face. He hoped it would mask his annoyance.

"Good morning, Mr. Ecto," Richard said, cheerfully. He already knew better than to extend his hand for a handshake. "I hope this morning finds you feeling better."

Alecto said something.

"Pardon me?

"Better," Alecto repeated, louder. "Yesss, I am feeling much better." *Now that my sisters are on their way.*

"Super," Richard said, genuinely relieved. He didn't like the idea of future fainting spells. "Well then, we'd better get going. They're waiting for us at the museum."

As they walked toward the exit, Richard couldn't help but notice the other guests staring at him and his strange companion.

The December day was unseasonably warm, even by California's standards. Richard would have made small talk about the weather, but attempts to talk about anything on the way to Mona's dinner last night all failed. Today he decided to let the classics channel on his XM radio fill the silence. He was grateful there were only around five miles between the hotel and the museum. Of course with LA traffic, the ten-minute trip could take an hour. Thankfully, because of Alecto's lateness, they missed the 405's notorious rush hour. Richard supposed he should be grateful.

They took the Sepulveda exit and turned right, following the signs to the Getty Center parking garage. Soon, Richard, Alecto, and several other visitors were on a tram that would take them for a brief, scenic ride up the hill to the Getty Center's entrance. It was a beautiful, white travertine building perched atop a hill in the Santa Monica Mountains.

In an understated but impressive way the building unfolded into view. No matter how many times Richard had seen it before, it never failed to affect him. He always figured the Center was as much a work of art as the art within it. Richard looked over at Mr. Ecto and thought he saw a pleased look on his face too. Alecto was only happy to be closer to her goal: the jar.

Because of their delay, they had to skip the architecture tour Richard had planned. The docent waiting for them at the arrival plaza took one look at Alecto and was relieved at the cancellation. Richard led Alecto to the East Building where the meeting for *The Ancients Alive* was already in progress.

"Forgive our tardiness," Richard said as he entered the room. "And, if you'll pardon our interruption, I'd like to introduce Mr. Al Ecto from Greece."

There was polite applause and impolite gawking. Richard sensed how awkward any greetings would be and made a move to avoid them.

"Mr. Ecto only arrived yesterday afternoon and has already been the unfortunate victim of a busy social calendar and jet lag. Let's do introductions another time, shall we?"

Richard motioned Alecto to the vacant seat near the front of the table where she clumsily sat down and bumped her knees.

"I won't ask Mr. Ecto to speak. We're already aware of his impressive expertise with Greek artifacts. As I said, it's been a rather difficult two days for him."

Alecto winced at the people smiling at her. For the first time, she was thankful for this no-nonsense man Richard. He was finally getting her. She hoped there would never come a time in the future when she'd have to torture him because of something horrible he did.

"I know we're all up to speed on our preview party tomorrow night, but can we walk through it for our esteemed guest here?"

One enthusiastic woman with spiky gray hair and red lipstick talked about a small music ensemble playing classical selections on the outdoor stage. Another petite, slight man requested a statement from Alecto for a press release for the Getty's media list. Another person, an older gentleman in a uniform, discussed security for that night. The exhibition's designer, a young hipster named Aaron, explained the layout and display.

Aaron stood over the exhibition's model and reviewed each section. After his extensive run-through, he breathed a heavy sigh.

"After all of that, there may be some last minute changes. Unfortunately, those potential changes affect a lot of other things."

Aaron went to work rearranging some walls and pedestals within the model.

"Like some of the art placements ... which, of course, means we have to move the corresponding information labels. That, of course, means we have to change the guided tour's audio narration."

Aaron sat back down in his chair and pulled on his goatee. The room was full of murmuring.

"If that's the case, we've already been in touch with Ms. Aniston's people. We have tentative studio time scheduled for her this evening and tomorrow morning."

Richard rubbed his tired eyes.

"What do you mean, 'some last minute changes', Aaron?" he asked. "The event is tomorrow. I'm not open to 'last minute changes.'"

"You won't believe this, Richard," Aaron said as he scratched his scruffy pork chop sideburns. "Last night a kid from facilities found a box tucked beneath some shelves while he was slinging his mop around in a storage room. It was labeled 'Ancient Greek' or something generic like that. Anyway, this kid may have accidently discovered the artifact of our lifetimes."

There were *oohs* and *aahs* from the people who didn't already know about the discovery. Alecto was herself intrigued and ceased the irritating drumming of her fingernails against the table to pay closer attention.

"Go on," Richard urged.

"Ann from research knows more about this than I do, but basically, we opened the crate and inside it was a jar."

Alecto sat straight up in her chair and bumped her knee on the glass tabletop, again. Pens, cups, and personal devices all jumped in response. Richard cleared his throat to regain the attention of the room.

"Just *a jar*?" he asked.

"Well, no, not just any jar. I mean, this thing is fairly big and very, terribly, *painfully* beautiful. I've seen it." Aaron went on, grinning. His excitement was obvious.

"Ann said that it clearly predates the Hellenistic period, but the relief on it is every bit as decorative as anything else during that era, if not more so. And, in spite of what we believe is its antiquity, the jar is in absolutely, uncommonly perfect condition. It's made of what appears to be marble, and get this, it has a cover that no one has been able to remove." Aaron was pleased with the looks of shock surrounding him.

"The relief. You said it has a relief," Richard interrupted, ignoring Aaron's excitement. "What does it show?"

"Oh man! That's the best part," Aaron smiled. "It shows the beginnings of the first woman ... according to Greek mythology anyway. It's the story of Pandora. One panel shows her creation from clay, another illustrates the gods in procession to her with all kinds of gifts, and on the uppermost panel there's her wedding to whom we can only presume is Epimetheus. It's totally wicked."

Alecto finally spoke. Loudly this time.

"Where is this jar?" she asked, though it sounded more like a demand.

"It's in security right now with some of our curators. They've been here since three o'clock this morning trying to figure out what this thing is and where it could have come from. No luck so far, but that might change here soon."

Aaron leaned back in his chair and laced his fingers behind his head.

"Tonight, Dr. Harish Nallapati is arriving from London to take a look at it. He's the senior curator of Ancient Greece at the British Museum. It's only right since they've partnered with us for the exhibition." Aaron looked around the room. "We might have a gem on our hands, people. This could be big."

"When can I sssee it? When can I see this jar?" Alecto insisted. She could almost feel it in her hands.

"Well now, let's not worry about the jar until we know what it is," Richard responded. "For all we know, this can be a hoax from our favorite missing curator, Mr. Ward. No? Maybe this is his final prank before leaving us out in the cold. While we're figuring this out, I'll take Mr. Ecto to the exhibition area for a walk-through and then he can prepare his gallery speech."

Richard stood at the table.

"Good work, everyone. Tomorrow evening's preview party is going to be something special, I can tell already."

Alecto got up to follow her host. The rest of the people in the meeting gave her a wide berth to pass. She started thinking, maybe this was for the best. She shouldn't attempt the jar until tomorrow night. It would be easier to get it with the help of her sisters and with the distraction of a large crowd of people.

Yes. This is for the best.

For the first time since Basanizo's death, Alecto started to feel like her former, vengeful self.

CHAPTER 28
VICTORY PRAYS FOR VICTORY

GABE CAME OVER after school. The friends acted like everything was as normal as it had ever been. They did homework, filled up on snacks, and then crashed on the couch for some TV. When the coast was clear, Charis told him about her visit with Athena and Hermes. She also told him the shiny, sparkly, glittery little keychain that dangled from her hip was one of the most impressive beings ever.

Rather, she *tried* to tell him about these things. She knew her words fell well short of what they actually represented. Charis had come to understand that when talking about gods, words alone weren't enough. One had to personally experience them, and even then one couldn't be sure.

Gabe told her about his conversation with Mr. P and about the epic meltdown Lauren had at lunch when she heard that Brady had asked Charis to the dance.

"It was probably a good thing you weren't at school today," he said with popcorn in his mouth.

All things considered, Charis would rather deal with a ballistic Lauren than a crazed Erinyes Sister.

The family plus Gabe had dinner—Chinese take-out. Neither Mona nor Evan felt much like cooking after last night. Gabe went home after dinner and Charis went to sleep. She felt exhausted after the day's events. Even though she had pretended to sleep all day, Charis excused herself to bed early. Her mom attributed it to a growth spurt. She was right, but not in the way she thought.

Charis brushed her teeth and dressed for bed. She placed Nike on the nightstand next to her.

"Tomorrow night's the night. Getty Museum, here we come," she said, trying to smile at the goddess. Charis felt the beginnings of the nervousness she was sure would follow her into her sleep and beyond. "Face-to-face with destiny and all of that."

"You're prepared. We've gone over the plan, and I'll be with you every step of the way," Nike promised.

Charis smiled hopefully at her guardian. She reminded herself how tall she had stood and how strong she was earlier with Athena and Hermes.

"You'll be with me every step of the way," she repeated. The clock only read eight-thirty, but Charis was overcome with sleep. "Good night, Nike."

"Good night, Charis." Before she knew what she was saying, Nike added, "I love you."

"I love you, too," Charis said in a yawn as she shut off her light.

In the dark, an uncharacteristic tear rolled from Nike's eye. She quickly wiped it away, as if trying to hide it from herself. She didn't mean to, and even tried not to, but yes, she had indeed fallen in love with Charis. How could she not? The girl was so brave. So smart. So trusting. Nike had never been this intimate with a human before, and Charis had taken her heart hostage.

Athena had warned the Warrior Goddess against softening toward Charis. She said becoming emotionally invested could compromise Nike's lone objective—to get the jar. Athena understood that Charis, her family, and her friends could all be placed in harm's way in the endeavor. It was easier to take risks with people for whom you cared a little than a lot. Athena feared that should Nike fall in love with the girl, she might not be able to do whatever was necessary to get her to the jar, including put the child in peril. Athena said the fate of mankind is greater than that of one individual. But Nike could see Athena's affection for Charis too. The Goddess of Wisdom had abandoned her head and followed her heart when it came to Charis. It was as though the girl had a way of overwhelming everything, including one's fears.

Nike flew over to the window and opened the curtains. Nyx, the Goddess of Night, cast her velvety canopy over the winter sky. Nike heard Charis sound asleep behind her. Looking at her own reflection in the window glass, Nike repeated the same prayer often prayed to her by brave warriors before a deadly battle:

"O powerful Nike, by men desired, with adverse breasts to dreadful fury fired, thee I invoke, whose might alone can quell contending rage and molestation fell. 'Tis thine in battle to confer the crown, the victor's prize, the mark of sweet renown; for thou rulest all things, Nike divine! And glorious strife, and joyful shouts are thine. Come, mighty goddess, and thy suppliant bless, with sparkling eyes, elated with success; may deeds illustrious thy protection claim, and find, led on by thee, immortal fame."

Nike looked to the heavens and prayed to the daughters of Zeus, the Litia, to hear her petitions. She prayed to them for strength to protect the girl. She prayed for the courage to confront her own fears. She prayed for fortune in the battle ahead. She prayed for victory. At this, she felt her own heart ignite in response.

It's already in you, Nike. You are the answer to your own prayer.

The goddess fluttered to Charis's pillow and quietly let herself down. She lay near the girl's face, so still with sound sleep, and eventually found her own.

Rest, Nike, for tomorrow, we do battle. But tonight, we rest.

Nike sank deeper into the pillow that cradled her whole little body.

CHAPTER 29
HADES SENDS HIS REGARDS

It was still dark. Charis got up from her bed and tiptoed to the bedroom window, careful not to wake Nike. She opened her laced curtains and couldn't believe her eyes. What a beautiful night! She'd never seen so many stars. Charis flung open the window as high as it would go and let the cool night air kiss her face. It felt so good, so inviting, that she climbed into the windowsill to take it all in. Charis looked down to her lawn at the glistening grass. It shimmered with dew in the moonlight, a carpet of little diamonds, sparkling just for her.

On a whim, Charis leapt from the window and dove into the grass below. The cold droplets of water felt like the ocean she loved so well. Charis roiled in the cool, crashing waves of the blue waters. Her body floated free as a jellyfish, like she hadn't a care in the world.

Charis kicked her way deeper into the chilly depths. It was as dark as the midnight sky dripping all around her. The velvety canvas brushed against her feathered wings as she beat them up and down to the rhythm of her own heart. Up, down, ba dump, ba dump. Up, down, ba dump, ba dump. Charis flew as fast as she could, enjoying every moment of wind in her hair and power in her wings.

As she soared through the heavens, Charis discovered she wasn't alone in the night sky. In a burst of warm light, a multitude of bright, laughing, dancing stars pierced through the dark. It was an explosion of the spectacular.

All around Charis, happy stars twinkled loudly to celebrate and honor the girl flying among them. Each flash of their light was a new round of applause. Charis felt like a star herself. She smiled at their adoration, delighted in their praise. This was special.

Finally, with voices befitting celestial beings, they sang a song in her honor. It was beautiful. It was grand. It was all about Charis and how wonderful she was. Even though she didn't know the enchanting melody lifting around her, Charis sang along anyway, belting every note as if she did.

In the middle of all of her carrying on—her head back, eyes closed, and mouth opened in raucous singing—Charis realized that all had gone quiet except for her voice alone.

The girl nervously looked around. The thousands of scattered stars, once her adoring friends, now stared at her in silence, glaring their disapproval. Without warning the stars opened their mouths and belched a low, long blast of sound. The eruption held everything in its grip. Charis clutched her hands to her ears and squeezed her eyes shut against the blaring.

The whole universe shook, rattling Charis along with it. Her teeth clattered in her head, her bones in her body, and her insides all over the place. Charis tightened her every muscle, trying to keep from breaking into a million pieces. When she thought she could stand no more, the stars stopped their ruckus and slammed their mouths shut. Charis braced herself for the worst she was sure would come. It did.

The stars grimaced, a threatening look of contempt. As Charis turned to flee, each star inhaled a deep, long breath, one after another. The silky black night disappeared into the blinding white light of the stars, one breath at a time. Planets and universes, galaxies and mysteries, all drained into their constant sucking and pulling. The world around Charis was becoming an awful blank nothing.

She felt the tug at her feet first, the tips of her toes vanishing into white. She tried to fly away, but the suction into the stars was strong. Her legs were beginning to fade ... now the tips of her wings. Charis strained with clinched teeth but the white continued to draw her in. Terror gripped her heart just as it was erased. Neck. Chin. Mouth. Nose. Charis's horror-stricken eyes were the last to disappear into the cold, colorless white that turned her dream into this nightmare.

Black. Now things were black.

Charis lay in a pile on the cold, damp ground. Her cheek pressed into the gray jagged stone beneath it. She peeled her eyes opened and moaned aloud. Her thoughts were as fuzzy as the tousled hair on her head.

"I had not known you were accustomed to laying prostrate before the gods." The voice growling above her had an audible sneer. "I was led to believe you fancied yourself so *familiar*, so *important*, that you simply strolled into our presence."

Charis's heart raced even though she lay as still as she could. She took a deep breath in and gagged at the taste the putrid air left in her mouth. The soft crying in the background played like a sad song. Charis knew exactly where she was, and with whom.

"Go on, girl. Get up. I know you're not bowed from devotion but from your defeat. Now, go on, *get up!*" Charis's rubbery legs shook with fatigue as she stood to see the figure sitting before her. "I am …"

"Hades," she finished, quickly lowering her gaze. She shouldn't have interrupted him.

"Yes. Yes, that's right." He leaned back against his throne and stroked his curly, black beard. "And, since you know so much, do you know why you are here?"

"I'm guessing it has something to do with Pandora's Jar," she whispered.

"Correct. But let me tell you, *girl*, there is much about the affairs that you meddle in that you know nothing about."

Hades rose from his throne and eased toward her, looking like a lion stalking his prey. Charis kept her eyes to the floor, not daring to look him in the face. As Hades circled her, Charis saw only his enormous feet.

"Little girls, no matter how highly they esteem themselves, have no business consorting with gods as though they are peers, as though they are friends."

Charis's face frowned. She wasn't the one who had started the "consorting." Before Athena began visiting her in dreams, Charis was happy to have the gods at a distance and behaving somewhat rationally within the pages of sacred books. After all, her life—changed, in danger, and now shrouded in mysterious prophesies—had been nothing but questions without real answers ever since. She wasn't any happier about this consorting business than Hades, but she didn't think this was a two-way conversation so she remained quiet.

"I've brought you here to warn you, child … *Charis* …Pah!" He said her name like it was a curse. It sounded nothing like when Hermes said it.

"Stay out of matters that don't concern you. Stay away from *things* that don't belong to you."

Hades's anger grew with every word. Charis nearly sliced the tip of her finger clean off, her hair was wrapped around it so tightly.

"I know some of the other gods among the pantheon have told you otherwise, but they are misguided in spite of their supposed wisdom and bravery and such. The truth is, none of this concerns you."

Hades stopped pacing and stood directly in front of Charis. She continued staring down at his feet, fidgeting nervously with a ringlet. When she last talked with Hermes and Athena, they were convinced that Hades didn't know that it was Hermes who took the jar. Clearly, as the angry god snarled above her, they were wrong.

Hades grabbed one of Charis's hands and squeezed it within his own. She gasped. Charis's eyes opened again as they had with Athena and with Mr. P, but this time, they opened to the dark. Charis went limp with feelings of misery and pain, of terror and anger. The eyes of her heart saw the present and future suffering of all of mankind. She saw the world as it would become if she didn't get the jar. Charis pulled her hand free and fell to the ground, shivering.

"Don't, please … don't," she tried to speak, but her words stopped in her throat. Instead she just cried.

"You have no destiny to keep! No history to make! No greater purpose than to continue in your plain life just like all of the rest of humanity."

Charis lifted her tear-stained eyes and stared brazenly into his black ones. She wanted to see if he looked as hateful as he sounded. He did.

"You are just a *child*, not a legend. A girl, not a prophecy."

His lip curled as he brought his face down to hers. Every word he spat was like a slap in the face.

"You know I'm right, don't you?" He stood tall above her and sighed a deep sigh. A smirk crossed his lips. "A legend! Why even you don't believe that, do you? No, no you don't. The truth is, Charis, it's just as you fear in your deepest, most secret thoughts. You, sadly, are most correct. You really are nothing special!" he shouted.

Spit escaped his mouth and landed on her face. His curses fell down on Charis just like the rain above baptizing her head, her arms, her shoulders, her wings, and legs.

Fat raindrops started to pelt her from the stormy sky overhead. Charis was getting soaked through. Shaking, she struggled to her feet and looked around for an escape. Charis couldn't see anything through the sheets of cold rain pouring down, not even Hades. She couldn't see him, but she heard him just fine.

"Do you hear me?" he yelled. "You are nothing special!"

Charis tried to run, but the rushing water was well above her knees and the force of it was too strong. She strained to lift her wings to fly, but they were too waterlogged and heavy like the pajamas she still wore. The sloshing water continued to rise. Charis slapped against the choppy waves to swim, but the current was strong and fast and fought against her, tossing her as it pleased.

Though Charis tried her best to keep her head above the flood, exhaustion claimed her every muscle. Soon, her panicked face submerged beneath the cold water. She looked this way and that for something, someone to rescue her, but saw nothing but the milky-blue ocean all around. Charis surfaced for a quick breath, kicking her legs wildly before slipping under again. Her lungs burned for air, her heart for home.

Home.

She fought her way to the surface once more.

"Help! Somebody! Help!" she cried. Her tears were indistinguishable from the relentless rain that continued to fall.

Charis yelled out again and breathed her final terrified breath before the angry water pulled her beneath its waves.

It was over. Charis was slipping away. She looked up at the surface of her watery tomb. It loomed a million unreachable miles above her. Charis stopped fighting and her body became still, weightless in the water that held it. Her eyes fluttered closed, peacefully. Flashing memories of her mother's hands playing in her tangled hair, her father's cologne surprising her in a breeze, and her brother's promises that she would always be his first girl flooded her mind. As Charis sank downward in her liquid grave, she thought about Gabe and how she loved him, and how that if they weren't just kids that might mean something more ... something forever. Charis resisted the urge to fight against the blackness overtaking her, instead she embraced the last thing she would remember : *I am something special.*

FRIDAY

You will never do anything in this world without courage. It is the greatest quality of the mind next to honor.

—ARISTOTLE

CHAPTER 30
CHOICES TO MAKE

SHE DIDN'T WANT TO, but she had to, so she did. And—given her size—it shouldn't have hurt, but it did hurt, because she's Nike.

"Wake *up!*" Nike pleaded as she slapped Charis's face with her little hands as softly she could. "Charis, you must wake *up!*" The goddess slapped her again.

Charis groaned as her eyes slowly opened. Warm tears streamed down into her ears and collected in pools there.

"Charis, you've had a dream. You're okay," Nike said hovering over her. "It was just a dream. I'm right here."

Charis focused her eyes and looked up at the blurry little goddess and sobbed some more. She mumbled some words that Nike tried to understand. She was flying. There were stars. Hades threatened her. She drowned in a flood. Nike wished she were larger so that she could cradle the girl.

Hades. So, Hades knows it was Hermes who took the jar.

Nike needed to tell Athena and Hermes. Immediately. This mission to get Charis to the jar just got a lot more complicated. Not only did they have Alecto to deal with, but likely her sisters too. And now, Hades.

So be it.

"You're okay, Charis. Come on. Come with me. I want you to see this."

Nike flew to the window and pulled the curtains wide. It was dawn and the sun was rising. Charis stood next to her, blinking her swollen eyes.

"Look at that! Helios, the God of the Sun, rides his sun chariot across the sky." Hues of yellow, orange, and red proclaimed the new day. "It's beautiful, isn't it?"

Charis couldn't appreciate the light, still haunted by the darkness she had just survived.

"Hades told me to stay out of this, Nike. He said it wasn't any of my business and that I should stay out of it." Tears filled Charis's eyes again. "And then he said that I was just some ordinary little insignificant child ... all this talk about 'destiny'!" She wiped her tears on the sleeves of her pajamas.

"He warned me, Nike. Hades warned me. And he is really pissed off. At me! What have I gotten myself into? What have *you* gotten me into? I didn't ask for any of this, Nike."

Nike continued to look at the sunrise and recited a hymn to Helios, the Sun God:

> "Hear, golden Titan, whose eternal eye with broad survey, illumines all the sky.
> Self-born, unwearied in diffusing light, and to all eyes the mirror of delight:
> Lord of the Seasons, with thy fiery car and leaping coursers, beaming light from far:
> With thy right hand the source of morning light, and with thy left the father of the night.
> Agile and vig'rous, venerable Sun, fiery and bright around the heav'ns you run.
> Foe to the wicked, but the good man's guide, o'er all his steps propitious you preside."

"That's beautiful, isn't it?" Nike asked. Charis remained silent, absent-mindedly twirling her hair around a finger.

"Charis, it is a new day." Nike turned around and fluttered directly in front of Charis's face. "Every time Helios races his chariot across the morning sky, it is another opportunity. With every sunrise, we get to choose ... who we are, what we believe, and how we will live the life the gods have given us. We can't always choose our circumstances. No. The Fates do that. But we can always choose who we will be and *how* we will be within them."

"Every day, we can make those choices however we wish and using whatever information we have. We can consult the constellations, our sacred books, and most especially, our very own hearts. We can choose from places of fear and doubt, or love and faith. But, and you must believe me when I say this, the choice is ours alone to make. No one can choose for another. We must each choose for ourselves."

Nike turned back to the window and watched Helios perform his every day miracle, so often ignored by the people, crops, and animals blessed by it.

"You can walk away from your journey to Pandora's Jar and you'd still be you—intelligent, kind, and brave. Or you can continue and see your journey to whatever end the Fates have in store. Either way, I want you to know that no matter what you choose, I love you still."

Charis stood behind Nike, choosing. She thought back to her nocturnal visit with Hades and hugged herself. She had been absolutely gripped in the hands of terror. Maybe what Hades said was true. Maybe this wasn't her business. Maybe all this talk about destiny was just that, talk. But there was something in her heart that told her otherwise. Whether or not she would *listen* to that something, Charis didn't know yet.

CHAPTER 31
A WILLING MESS

EVEN THOUGH she did everything she could to stay positive, the day just kept getting worse. After her morning shower, Charis wrote her word of the day in the bathroom mirror. She was thoughtful, perhaps more so than ever before. This was, after all, an important day. One that, like Nike reminded, was up to her to live as she chose. After some soul searching, Charis decided she was willing to see this jar business to the end. She was willing to trust her heart. She was willing to pursue her destiny. She was willing to leave the consequences to fate. She had willingness within, urging her onward in spite of her fear. In the foggy mirror, she wrote, 'a willingness to try'. Yes. That felt right.

It was when she went back into the bathroom after getting dressed that she saw her 'n' looked more like an 'm'. The words she had conjured to shape her day actually read, "a willing 'mess' to try." She stared at it with disgust before erasing the faint accusation from the mirror with her sleeve. She hoped it wasn't a portend of things to come.

If that wasn't bad enough, at breakfast, Charis's mom told her that she'd invited Alecto to the school play that afternoon. "I thought it would smooth things over. Maybe explain a little better where you were coming from with Pandora's Jar. He seemed so upset about it."

Charis railed against her mother in a shocking rant.

I don't want that weirdo at my school! He smells funny! The kids will make fun of me! Blah! Blah! Blah!

But, it was too late. The invitation was already extended and surprisingly accepted.

The rest of the conversation from Charis's mom went something like ... "And, what's more, you had better get your attitude together, young lady, before you get yourself into trouble."

Charis smoldered at her mom, unable to restrain her fear and anger.

"I'm already *in* 'trouble,' damn it! Argh!" Charis slammed her hand on the breakfast table, stunning her mom, dad, and Presley into silence. Her heart sank as she looked at their faces. She was becoming the ugly that she was supposed to fight, to stop.

"God!" she shouted to the sky as she grabbed her backpack and ran outside to her front porch where she waited for Gabe ... who was late. Ten minutes late.

Charis was walking by herself when he came running up from behind.

"Sorry," he said, breathing heavily. Gabe's hair stuck to his forehead with sweat. "The dog barfed everywhere and I had to clean it up. It was so gross." Charis remained silent, her eyes to the ground. "You okay?"

"Yeah, sure. I'm fine. Can't you tell?" she snapped.

"Whoa ... what did I do? I just got here." Gabe was right. He hadn't done anything to deserve her daggers. No one had.

"Nothing," she said. "I'm sorry. It's already been an awful morning, that's all." She told him about her mom inviting Alecto to the play this afternoon. She didn't tell him about her willing mess.

"Oh, man." Gabe complained. "That freak is coming to school? I can see why you're so crabby." Charis shot him a look. "I'm sorry. I just meant I understand why you're stressed out." Gabe looked at Nike hanging from Charis's backpack. "It's going to be okay though. We have Tinker Bell on steroids on our side." That put a smile on Nike's face, but Charis gloomed on.

"Speaking of," Charis remembered, "at some point I need to find a place where *Tinker Bell* can talk with Athena and Hermes. Somewhere private, where they won't be seen."

"Why? What's up?"

"I had a dream last night … more like a nightmare. Hades was there."

"Really? Hades? Crap! What happened?"

A lot of things had happened, but what bothered Charis most about the nightmare was Hades calling her "nothing special." She didn't want to tell Gabe about that, afraid it would reveal her insecurities that it just might be true; that maybe the other gods picked the wrong girl.

"Let's just say the God of the Underworld isn't exactly someone you want to piss off, and I have. Nike's got to talk with the others to figure out what to do if I'm going to have any chance of surviving this mess and getting the jar so the rest of the world does too."

"Well, I'm sure Mr. P can work that out, right?" Gabe asked. "Hey, do you think I can be there this time?" Charis looked at Nike and she shrugged her shoulders.

"Sure, but be quiet and don't say anything stupid. All right?"

"When have I ever …" Gabe started. "Never mind."

* * *

Charis and Gabe hadn't been on campus more than two minutes before …

"Well, looky who decided to show up for school today. It's Charis."

The way Lauren said her name reminded Charis of Hades. Lauren and the other Harpies had blocked Charis's path and were standing in front of her with their arms folded in exactly the same way. It looked like they were about to break into a well-choreographed flash mob. Lauren scowled at Charis, but the hapless girl had no idea that today wasn't the best day to pick a fight. Today, Charis felt anything but jealous, intimidated, or concerned about the middle-school drama glaring at her with her arms crossed. She had more pressing things on her mind like monsters, gods, and the fate of the world, for which she felt largely responsible.

"What do you want, Lauren?" Charis asked bluntly. "What could you possibly want with me?"

Lauren's eyebrows rose in surprise, but only briefly. Her eyes soon squinted into a frown meant to scare the crap out of Charis. The queen of middle school wasn't used to being talked to with such disregard. Lauren took a finger and pointed it and her bright orange nail polish in Charis's face, living up to the reputation of mean girls everywhere.

"You know what I want!" she said through clinched teeth. "I want you to apologize! I know you tried to ruin my dance by throwing yourself at Brady." She inched closer to Charis. "And, I know you practically begged him to ask you to the dance, too." Charis wondered how words could escape from such a tightly pinched mouth. "He only asked you to the dance because he felt sorry for you! But it doesn't matter anyway because *I* will be going to the dance with him tonight and you won't! You lose, Charis. You lose!"

Before she knew it, Charis did lose … *it*. Her very own, personal Pandora's Jar sprang open and all of the anger and fear of the past few days broke free. Charis lunged for Lauren, unsure of what exactly she planned to do when she reached her. To her surprise, Charis found herself stuck and unable to move. It was Nike. As the little goddess hung innocently from Charis's backpack, she discretely flapped her wings and fought against the girl's momentum to keep her away from Lauren.

Charis continued to struggle toward Lauren anyway, her arms reaching forward while her shoulders strained back. It looked weird, like she was one of those old-fashioned marionettes hanging from tangled strings. Gabe saw Nike flapping her wings like the wind and ran over to Charis to pretend he was the one restraining her.

"You're right! You win! I lose!" Charis yelled, pulling against her backpack. While Charis reached forward, Lauren stepped back, appalled. "Does that make you happy? Does it?" Charis grunted. "Oh, forget it!"

Exhausted, she finally stopped struggling against Nike and bent over, hands to knees, to catch her breath.

"Yes. Yes, I wanted to go to the dance with Brady. Of course I did. So what. Doesn't everybody?" She stood up and stared Lauren face-to-face. "*Everybody*, Lauren," she continued. "Including your clone friends standing behind you. And, why not? He's a great guy! He's smart. He's nice. He's hot. Why wouldn't I want to hang out with him? I'm not stupid!"

Kids ran off of their busses toward the action and a crowd gathered around the two girls.

"You're right about that. But you're wrong about all the rest. I didn't throw myself at Brady. I wouldn't do that for him or anyone else. And, no, I didn't *beg* him to ask me to the stupid dance. I think he's smart enough to make up his own mind. You do too, obviously, and that's why you tried to pressure him into asking you to the dance, right? You knew he was going to ask me and you couldn't have that, could you? No! So you tried to make up his mind for him. What tha? And *I'm* the pathetic one? Please!"

Charis paused to calm down. She needed to catch up with herself. She was *so* mad, and expressing it so freely felt kind of good. That scared her.

"But none of it matters anyway. I can't go to the dance, Lauren. I can't. I'm going to be busy doing something waaaaay more important with a friend who is *as* great, *as* smart, *as* nice, and *as* hot!"

She darted a look at a very bright red Gabe. He smiled. He couldn't help it.

"So quit worrying about me, okay? Go. Get a dress or something. Put on some lip gloss and have fun dancing with someone who chose you second!" Charis could almost hear Pandora's spirit of jealousy chuckling in her ear and it sent chills up her spine. She felt horrible.

Applause erupted from the circle of students surrounding the two girls. Lauren had never been so embarrassed in her life. She loved being the center of attention, but not this kind. It seemed like the whole school was there, looking at her like she had mud on her face. Every classmate she'd ever wronged—and even some she hadn't—stood cheering and clapping for Charis. When Charis saw the look of heartbreak find Lauren's face, her own heart hurt too. Charis reached out to apologize, but Lauren took off before she could, crying. Her entourage stayed behind, not knowing what to do.

"Great," Charis huffed, throwing her hands in the air. "This is just great. I'm a real jerk." The teachers who had made their way over to the commotion broke things up and told kids to get to class before they were all marked tardy.

"Come on, Charis," Gabe said. He put his hand on her shoulder. "This wasn't your fault. She asked for that one." Andy came up nodding her agreement. When Charis turned to go to class she bumped right into Brady. He had been standing close behind her the whole time.

Could this get any worse?

"I'm … I'm sorry." She didn't know what she was apologizing for, but it felt like the right thing to do.

"No," he responded. "I'm the one who's sorry." Brady asked if he could walk Charis to class so Gabe and Andy left the two of them alone.

"I don't know about Lauren sometimes. I mean, she's a great friend, but that's all she is. I don't like her like a girlfriend or anything, and believe me, I've told her that a million times. She just doesn't get it though. I'm sorry. She really flipped out on you, huh?"

"It's not your fault. She's responsible for her own actions. And, so am I. I guess I was pretty harsh with her just now. It's just, I've had a bad morning already … I've got a lot on my mind."

"I understand. You don't need to explain yourself, Charis. And, like I said the other day, maybe next dance? If you want."

"Sure. Of course," Charis smiled.

"Sorry again, Charis. I didn't realize I'd get you into such a mess." He smiled openly and Charis thought she just might catch on fire.

It was, at least, a *willing* mess.

* * *

Students involved with the play were dismissed from their first period classes so they could have one final rehearsal. Before the first bell rung, kids were already in costume, rehearsing lines, and making last-minute changes to the set.

"Okay, class," Mr. P said. "This is it! This is the big day!" He had a broad smile on his face. "We're going to knock 'em dead! Right?" There were hoots and hollers from all around the auditorium. "We have time for a quick run-through before we're live, so everyone take your places."

After a few seconds of scrambling, everyone was ready and the house lights went down. Charis, Gabe, and Brady all sat in the back row, watching. After the chorus marched past, Charis excused herself to talk to Mr. P.

"Hey, Charis," he said. "It's good to see you. We missed you in class yesterday, but I understand you had some important matters to attend to." His eyes twinkled an understanding.

"Are you ready?"

She didn't know if he meant for the play, round two with Lauren, or confronting her worst fears later at the museum. It didn't matter. She was approaching this day with a willing mess for whatever it held, right?

"Sure," she shrugged. "I have to talk to you though. There've been some … some changes." She stood on tiptoes to whisper in his ear and told him about her dream with Hades. "Nike needs to talk to your mom and Hermes. Where can we go to do that?" Mr. P thought about it.

"Well, the whole school will be in the auditorium in …" he looked up at the clock on the wall, "forty-five minutes. So, anywhere but here, I guess." He reached into his pockets and pulled out his keys. He picked one from among the others and gave it to Charis. "This will get you into my classroom. Just draw the shades, okay?"

"Of course," she said.

"And, make it fast. I don't want anyone to notice you're not here." Charis thought about her mom and Alecto coming. Alecto coming!

"Mr. P, I forgot to tell you. Alecto. She's coming to the play!"

"Super," he said, surprisingly. "Then let's give her a great show."

CHAPTER 32
THE DOCTOR IS IN

DR. NALLAPATI STOOD beneath the bright fluorescent lights analyzing the exquisite jar. He held the magnifying glass to his brown eyes again. It was unlike anything he'd ever seen. The sculpting had clearly been done by an expert … the likes of the Great Phidias, but more elegant. He bent closer to it and squinted his eyes. He couldn't quite place the tools that were used, the lines were so fine.

Ah, well.

There was *much* about the jar the doctor didn't know except for the obvious … that it was wonderfully sculpted. Whoever this artist was, Dr. Nallapati had not encountered his work before in the over forty-five years of his career.

He traced his gloved fingers over the relief of Pandora. Her gown clung to her body as if pushed against her by wind. Its folds were deep and fluid and many. The skirt appeared to be at the start or end of a twirl. And, her face. Pandora's face. Such details. Such an emphasis on individual features. Wide-set eyes. Upturned nose. Full lips. Rounded cheeks. The fine details were greater than anything from the Roman Period when all those self-important emperors insisted on accurate representation. Whoever sculpted Pandora fashioned a perfect creature.

Dr. Nallapati took a step back. Richard, Aaron, and a few others waited for him to say something, *anything*, to let them know what they had on their hands. Was it a hoax or the greatest find since King Tut's tomb?

"Say there, can you shut the lights once more?" he asked. His British accent gave an air of formality. The lights went out and only the glow from the black lamp shone. Under its light, the jar was a determined blue.

"Brilliant." Dr. Nallapati said to himself. "It's simply brilliant, now isn't it?" He touched it again with his gloved hands. "That'll do. Thanks." At last, he turned to the attentive small crowd.

"Ladies and gentlemen," Dr. Nallapati said. "I'm afraid I haven't a clue." A collective sigh of disappointment followed.

"Wait, wait ..." he urged. "Before your spirits are completely dashed, there are some things I can safely assume." He looked down at the jar and used his finger as a pointer.

"The relief suggests to me that it's as authentic as the Elgin Marbles. It's perfect, but not overly, symmetrically so. It was, doubtless, carved by a master ... likely from the Pergamene school. Though, I've not seen work of this caliber from there or elsewhere for that matter. I believe the marble is Thasin, though I cannot be certain without further testing. And, as evidenced by its blue coloration beneath the black lamp, it appears authentically aged. Ancient really. But," he said, his finger now pointed in the air, "this jar lacks any other evidence of aging whatsoever. For example, there is absolutely no patina anywhere." There were murmurs throughout the room.

"And, that is the problem, isn't it? When was this piece made? A month ago, by a talented charlatan? Or 400 BC by a previously undiscovered master? Stylistically, it points to the Hellenistic Era. There," he said, pointing once more. "Look at the hips on this one. I believe she is Aphrodite. See how they are positioned? They are twisted. She has the Hellenistic twist. But, the story on the vase is more archaic, don't you agree? God themes. Mythology. The Greeks were mostly done with that by the time the Hellenistic Era came around."

Dr. Nallapati walked to the other side of the jar, his footsteps echoing in the room. "And, what of its function? It's a nice size, and made of marble. It's heavy, but certainly one person could manage if there were nothing inside. This jar couldn't have been meant to carry water like a hydra jar. It would be too heavy. And yet, clearly, *clearly* it was meant to hold something or there would not be this unyielding top." He tapped his finger to the side of his nose, pondering.

"So?" Richard asked, exasperated.

"So, I don't know," he sighed. Dr. Nallapati bit his lip, trying to keep his next words inside. He was unsuccessful.

"Colleagues, casting off science and reason, which is not my personal or professional habit, I have a hunch this jar deserves the extra study and careful handling it's asking for. I can't explain it." The doctor continued against his good judgment. "But ... but, if I were to revisit the boyhood notions that first compelled my study of art and antiquity, I would be giddy with the possibility that we may have stumbled upon Pandora's fabled jar, crafted perfectly by Hephaestus himself. Of course, I know it's ridiculous ..."

Richard shook his head. Yes, it was ridiculous. He couldn't take it anymore.

"Aaron, have a simple information card made for the jar. Have it read something like, I don't know, 'Unknown object. Unknown origin. Expert depiction of the myth of Pandora.' Consult one of the curators. They'll know what it should say. Cancel Ms. Aniston's studio time. It won't be necessary because we won't be adding this jar to the collection. We'll just tuck it somewhere in the back toward the end of the exhibition for tonight. We can certainly pull it before the exhibition goes public, but it might be fun for this crowd. We'll see."

Dr. Nallapati had already returned to studying the jar.

"Thanks for your time, Dr. Nallapati." Richard said, tapping the doctor on the shoulder and extending his hand for a handshake. "We'll have a car pick you up from your hotel at five o'clock this evening."

"Yes, yes," he murmured in response.

He turned his back toward Richard and tried to twist the top off of Pandora's Jar again. It wouldn't budge. Richard thought this guy was as strange as Mr. Ecto. Speaking of Mr. Ecto, Richard wondered if he might have provided more information about the jar than the doctor had. He almost regretted that the odd fellow wasn't there.

Nah.

It was probably good that Mr. Ecto had gone with Mona to the school play. It was certainly good for Richard that he had less time to be around him.

CHAPTER 33
THE SHOW MUST GO ON

MONA AND ALECTO took their seats in the auditorium. Alecto sat on the aisle so she could stretch at least one of her long legs. "Mr. Ecto" was a man of few words, so Mona was grateful for the other parents seated around her to chat with. The car ride from his hotel to Charis's school had been very silent.

After the first hellos, Mona stood at her seat looking for Charis. There were students, teachers, and proud family members milling around everywhere, but her daughter was nowhere to be found. After the way Charis had stormed out of the house that morning, Mona was more than a little worried about her. She would feel better if she could just lay eyes on her little girl, but the lights flickered off and on, signaling the start of the play.

Principal Lund spoke a brief welcome and then the lights went dark. Mona was glad. All of the open staring from the younger students at Alecto made her uncomfortable, though she understood it. Mr. Ecto *was* a strange looking man.

The chorus began their speaking procession to the stage from behind the audience. Students "ooh-ed" and "aah-ed" at the masks. There was some laughter when one of the kids from the chorus got tangled in his robe and fell to the floor, but he quickly recovered.

On cue, Zeus came to the stage and made a bold speech while the chorus echoed their parts. Mona looked at Alecto. She looked, surprisingly, engaged. Another actor, one heavily costumed with tools, joined Zeus on stage.

"Hephaestus," Zeus shouted. "God of fire and craft, with your hands and tools you shine. Make a woman, fair and bright, as lovely as a bride."

Zeus left the stage and, without a word, Hephaestus dropped to his knees and pretended to handle clay on the ground while the chorus twirled around in circles in front of him.

The chorus chanted:

"O workman, Hephaestus, what a work you do,

The fate you do not know.

The woman that you make of clay

Will bring us tears and woe."

The chorus split and went to either side of the stage, leaving a surprised and newly created Pandora standing in the center beneath a spotlight.

* * *

Charis and Gabe slipped out of the auditorium before the doors opened for the performance. They stole to Mr. P's room undetected. Charis knew her mother would be looking for her, but Nike had to talk to Hermes and Athena, so she had to risk it.

"Hurry," Gabe urged, looking left and right, his hair a mess.

"I'm trying!" Charis huffed inserting the key into the lock.

When they got into the classroom, they kept the lights off and ran to each window, closing the blinds. Nike unhooked herself from Charis's backpack.

"You know what to do," she said.

Charis quickly grabbed Gabe by the hand and pulled him to the opposite side of the room. They turned their backs to Nike and leaned on a closet door.

"Athena. Hermes. Come." Charis could picture in her mind what Nike was doing.

"Athena. Hermes. Come." There was a small vibration in the room. Gabe shot Charis a look but she motioned for him to close his eyes.

"Athena. Hermes. Come."

He didn't see it, but he sure did feel it. A warm burst of air blew Gabe into the closet door. He bumped his head a little. Charis quickly reached out and touched his hand to get his attention before he turned around. She smiled at him. She knew this was going to knock his socks off.

* * *

Zeus returned to the stage, his mask a little crooked, and examined Hephaestus's work. A sweet girl named Monica played Pandora, and she looked every bit of the part even without her mask.

"Almost perfect," Zeus said, triumphant. He ran from one side of the stage to the other, pretending to call someone from far away.

From the sides of the stage, the chorus began:

"The Olympians came from far and wide,

Their gifts to bestow on this lovely bride ..."

Middle-school masked gods entered from stage left and right, each holding items in their hands.

"They brought jewels and crowns, rubies and gowns ..."

As they passed Pandora, they placed the items at her feet.

"Presents of every sort.

Wisdom and cunning, intelligence and language,

The gift of gab and retort."

* * *

When Gabe turned around, he didn't know where he was, only *that* he was. He stumbled from the disorientation. Charis reached out to steady him, as if balance and not perspective was his problem. Before he could ask her where they were, she went running toward the gods. Gabe wanted to run too but he didn't know if he was on solid ground. Instead, he just watched Charis and hoped she didn't fall. The three shining things surrounded Charis in their light. After a few moments, or an eternity, Charis came back to retrieve her dumbstruck friend. She pulled him by the hand toward the lights and he stumbled behind her.

"Gabe," she said. "You know Nike."

No. No he didn't. There was a time when he thought he did, but, no.

"It's a pleasure to *properly* meet you, Gabe." When the goddess said "properly," Nike gestured her hands up and down the full length of her body. Her actual body, not the 4-inch version of it Gabe knew. He just stood there, saying nothing. He remembered that he'd insulted Nike. He questioned whether she'd be able to protect his friend. He felt ashamed of himself for that now and looked to the floor.

Charis shoved him a bit. "And, this is Athena."

"H~How do you do?" Gabe's voice cracked.

"Very well, Gabe," Athena smiled. "We can't thank you enough for the support you've been to our Charis." Athena extended her hand to his and he took it. He didn't know what to do with it because he'd never held a goddess's hand before, so he kissed it and promptly dropped it back to her side. Charis snickered.

"And, I'm Hermes." The muscular god standing before him reached out his hand to Gabe too. As Gabe grabbed it, he said, "No need to kiss mine, friend, unless you want to."

There was a warmth in his voice that put Gabe at ease. He felt like when his parents were still married and happy, and they all watched Monday Night Football together, rooting for the 49ers. Gabe wanted badly to go back there. Standing with three gods, he almost believed it possible even though his father had already assured him it was absolutely not.

"I know it is unusual that I've called you here," Nike said, looking from her fellow gods to the two kids with her. "But, something unusual has come up and it can't be ignored."

"Go on," Athena urged.

* * *

The chorus circled Pandora, hand in hand:

"They named her Pandora, all-gifted one,
And with one final gift from Zeus ..."
Zeus handed Pandora a jar.
"To the earth she was sent, and willingly went
To marry the Titan Epimetheus."

Pandora spun around in a circle, waving an arm up and down as if traveling by some unknown means until Epimetheus finally entered the stage. He was clearly late, and Pandora was clearly dizzy. Epimetheus's robe hung loosely from his body as he fumbled to tie on his belt. There were giggles from the audience.

The chorus continued:

"His brother, Prometheus, did warn him about Zeus
And advised him no gifts to receive,
But Epimetheus was smitten and he did not listen
And so the Titan was deceived.
In his arms he received the woman he believed
Was a gift from Olympus afar.
His love he declared though he should have been aware
Of the trickery that lived in her jar."

Epimetheus took Pandora in his arms and hugged her.

* * *

"Hades visited Charis in a dream last night," Nike said, gravely.

Both Athena and Hermes looked surprised.

"In no uncertain terms, Hades knows everything he needs to know to create trouble in Mt. Olympus. He knows Hermes took the jar and he knows that Charis communes with us." Nike put her hand on Charis's shoulder. "He has leveled a threat upon this child. He has issued her a warning."

"How ..." Athena started, then stopped. "The Helm of Darkness. He must have spied us talking with one another from Hermes's temple." She shook her head. "We should have known. He's full of trickery. But ... he leveled a threat? On an innocent?"

The room turned humid, sticky, and thick, as if rain clouds had snuck in beneath the classroom door. "Then he has issued a threat against me. Against us," Hermes said. His voice was the pounding of a million fists in the air.

"Temperance, Hermes," Athena chided. She bent her knees so that she was eye to eye with Charis. "Dear one, can you tell me what he said? How did you meet him?"

Charis told her about the dream, the grass, the sky, the stars, the vacuum, and the conversation she'd had with the God of the Underworld that resulted in a flood. She didn't start crying until she retold the part about him calling her "nothing special." Charis hated that it bothered her so. What did she care what Hades thought of her? Still, it made her so upset, and she wished it didn't. Athena saw how Hades's words pierced into Charis's doubt, and she couldn't refrain from hugging the girl. She was getting far more emotionally involved with this child than she ever intended to or thought she could.

"You don't need to be told this. And, certainly not from me. But you are something special, Charis." The girl's tears moved Athena from neutrality to anger. She knew that wasn't a good place from which to make decisions, so she took several deep breaths before speaking again. She stood up and turned to Hermes.

"Hermes ..."

"I know, I know. I must come to the earth as a human." He said. His words were bright and sharp. "Only, what deal can I make with the Fates this time? What do I have to give in exchange for their help?" He thought about the great sacrifice of tears Athena had already made with them to get Nike here. What more could there be?

* * *

There was a flood of red lights as Pandora took center stage alone. She gripped the jar in her hand. Off stage, the chorus shouted:

"Pandora! The jar! The jar! Don't open the jar,
For inside it lives heartache and pain.
But she was curious, terribly inquisitive,
And imagined there was wealth to gain."

The lights began to flash black and white, a warning of the soon-coming storm of evil upon the earth.

"With a twist of the lid from the jar did fly
A plague on the earth and all mankind.
Out sprung jealousy, greed, and pride,
Hate, fear, pain, and crime."

A member of the chorus slithered, crawled, or crept back on stage with every evil named, this time wearing red, terrible masks.

"In horror, she watched as the spirits took flight
To descend upon the earth the evil they might.
Taking hold of the jar, the lid she shut tight
Lest more wickedness be loosed and freed to smite
But there remained one spirit inside ..."

* * *

Athena could conjure nothing from the depths of her wisdom that they might offer the Fates in exchange for their help. Nothing. The three gods grappled for a solution. Hades would, undoubtedly, use his Helm of Darkness again should he attempt to fulfill his threat. But, what of Hermes? They talked back and forth, trying to discover a means for Hermes to travel to Gaia.

* * *

The chaos of writhing middle grade monsters flopping about on the stage came to a stop. A single white light shone on the jar Pandora held in her hands. The chorus knelt on their knees. An unmasked actor dressed in all black walked onto the stage and took his place next to Pandora. The student began reciting popular headlines of recent news. He announced roadside bombings in Iraq. He shouted the number of casualties lost to famine and drought. He listed diseases of every kind. He read the names of leaders and politicians scandalized into resignation. The audience listened, somber. Alecto shifted in her seat as the stage went black.

*   *   *

It dawned on him. He had an idea.

"Excuse me," Gabe interrupted. Charis shushed him. He frowned and continued. "Hey, guys ... um, gods, I, I have an idea." They stopped talking and waited.

"Well, and I don't know, but Hermes might not need to change when he gets here. To the earth, I mean."

"Of course he does, Gabe!" Charis replied, annoyed. "Look at him!" She motioned toward the glowing, sterling-silver-haired, preternaturally beautiful, tall, near-naked, chiseled god standing before them. "He doesn't exactly fit in. He doesn't even look real, for Pete's sake!"

"I know! Exactly!" Gabe said. "And what better way to hide than in plain sight at a Greek exhibition in a museum among other gods made of marble and gold?"

"Genius!" Charis shouted, herself messing up his hair. Gabe puffed out his chest a little bit.

"He's right," Nike said. "The boy is right." Athena smiled and nodded her approval. Hermes walked over to Gabe and placed his hand on his shoulder. Before he even spoke a word, Gabe felt his praise.

"Gabriel. You share your name with one of the noblest beings I know. I speak of the angel Gabriel, who faithfully acts as a divine messenger, heralding wisdom and hope to mankind. Today, you have done the same for me. Gabriel. Your name means 'God is my strength.' Today, you have strengthened me."

"Thank you, sir ... I mean ..."

"Hermes, you can call me Hermes. Or you can call me friend."

Gabe's confidence grew.

"Hey, I've got another idea! Nike, why don't you do it too? I bet Hades and those Erinyes Sisters would freak out to see *both* of you standing there out in the open, so big and ready to fight!"

"What? What's wrong?" Charis asked. "I think it's a great idea." She'd noticed the sad look exchanged between Nike and the others.

"Nothing, Charis. Nothing's *wrong*. I just can't do that," Nike said.

"Why not?"

"I can't change back into my true form until after you get the jar, that's all."

"What do you mean, Nike? You're big right now."

"Yes. I know that's how it appears, but it's only because we're 'praying'. When I talk with the gods like this—with me here, and them there—it's a lot like what humans do when you pray. In that moment of connection, you're able to see yourselves more clearly, as you truly are. The same is true for me, right now. But, when this time of communion is over, I'll be as before. It's the deal we made with the Fates. I'll return to my true self once our mission is complete."

"What tha? Nike! What have you done? What if I can't get the jar? You'll be stuck like this forever! That's not fair!" Charis hugged Nike close.

* * *

Both the stage and house lights were raised and the audience squirmed uncomfortably in their seats. The chorus returned to the stage without their costumes, wearing no masks or togas at all. Looking into the faces of their classmates, teachers, and families, they recited their final poem:

"In the world that we share there is trouble and woe
There is heartache and sadness, there is pain we all know
Pandora, poor Pandora, such remorse did she show
Such resolve to make right the wrong that she sowed."

Pandora unmasked herself, took off her robe, and walked down stage. She addressed the audience for the first time:

> *"The trouble I caused I could not foreknow*
> *But I do believe good can still follow*
> *If together we work for a better tomorrow*
> *If love is our guide and service our motto*
> *Then evil we will conquer, I know it to be so*
> *For here in my jar, we always have hope."*

Pandora opened her jar, dug her hand inside, and flung silver confetti out into the audience. It was a thunderous applause! Everyone stood to his or her feet. Everyone, except Alecto.

Foolish kids. Is this what they think? Is this where the child Charis got the notion that Hope must be released? What fools!

The gods knew what would happen if Hope was released. Mankind would exterminate itself. And that's what Nike, Hermes, and Athena wanted. They've been offended and ignored by man too long for their egos to suffer more disgrace. And the girl was helping them. It was unbelievable!

* * *

As he made his rounds through the school, the security guard sensed something funny walking behind Mr. P's classroom. He couldn't explain it. It just felt odd, like biting into an apple and tasting an orange. As he walked toward the room, he noticed the blinds were drawn. That was strange too. He pressed his ear to the classroom door and heard murmuring inside. The whole school was at the assembly, or so he thought. While he sifted through the hundreds of keys on the keychain, he noticed a bright light streaming out from beneath the door, so he sifted a little faster.

It was Nike, of course, who first heard the jingle of the keys. She looked to Athena and Hermes. "You must go. We must stop. Now!" Charis didn't want them to leave. She wanted to solve Nike's dilemma.

She wanted to come up with a plan. She needed Athena and Hermes to stay and help figure things out.

"No ..." the girl pleaded.

"Charis," Nike firmly chided, holding the girl's face in her hands. "For you, for the world, I'd do it again. It's what I chose. *My* destiny. *My* fate. You have your own to attain and live. Let's simply get the jar, okay? I need you to be brave."

Charis reluctantly nodded yes.

Athena and Hermes kissed Nike upon her cheek and vanished.

"Follow me," the now pocket-sized version of Nike whispered into the room that was now pitch black. Gabe stumbled through the dark, his eyes unadjusted, and loudly kicked over a chair.

"Crap," he cringed.

"Who's in there?" the security guard called.

Nike flew toward a storage closet and wielded her sword. She stabbed the lock and popped it open. "Quick, inside!" she whispered.

The classroom door swung open. The guard turned on the light and saw that the room was empty. He walked toward the overturned chair and set it right. He shrugged his shoulders. He must have imagined things.

Well, I might as well stay a minute.

The guard wanted to take a seat, close his eyes, and sit there with a smile on his face. So, that's what he did.

"What's he doing?" Gabe whispered, peering through the tiny slats of the closet door.

"Our presence," Nike said. "He's enjoying what's left of our presence."

Charis tiptoed behind Gabe so she could see. "Well, he'd better hurry, enjoy it, and move on. We've got to get out of here." It was hot in the small closet, and Charis was starting to feel claustrophobic. She moved to get more comfortable and accidentally bumped the wall with her elbow. The noise snapped the guard out of his reverie and he glanced over at the closet door.

"Noooo," whispered Charis.

"What'll we do now?" Gabe moaned. "Oh God, my dad's gonna go ballistic over this one. I'm caught in the closet, with you!"

As the guard closed in on the door, Nike attached herself to Charis's keychain. There was nothing she could do without blowing her cover. Just as the guard reached for the closet door, the bell ending second period sounded. Two wild kids ran down the hall cursing at one another, catching the guard's attention.

"Marc! Bryan! Come here, you two!" The guard ran from the room, closing the door after him. Charis, Gabe, and Nike all breathed a sigh of relief.

"The play! It must be over. We need to get to the auditorium fast before my mother knows I'm missing." Charis said.

They bolted from the closet and out of the room. Students began filling the hallways as the two friends ran through the crowd. They rounded the corner toward the entrance of the auditorium and ran smack into Mona and Alecto.

"Hey, we've you two been?" Mona asked. "We waited for you at our seats, but …"

"Backstage," Charis interjected. "We just ran from backstage." She was breathless, and a little bothered at how easy it was to lie to her mother, again. This wasn't something she wanted to get good at.

"Kids, you remember Mr. Ecto," Mona said. She ran her fingers through Charis's wind-swept hair, attempting to smooth it like this time it might actually work.

"Mr. Ecto," Charis said more bravely than she actually felt.

Alecto was about to speak when Mr. P walked up.

"Mrs. Parks. I'm Charis's teacher, Mr. Papadakis. It's a pleasure to finally meet you. I want to let you know what a star your daughter is in class. She's taken such a keen interest in Greek mythology. She's a real pro at it."

"Oh, why thank you. She's spoken highly of you as well." Mona looked at Mr. Ecto. He had the strangest expression on his face.

"Forgive my manners. Mr. Papadakis, this is Mr. Al Ecto. He's helping us out with the Greek exhibition at the Getty Museum. I'm sure Charis has told you all about it."

Alecto couldn't believe it, though it only confirmed her fears.

*Erichthonius! So Athena **was** involved.*

Erichthonius extended his hand to Alecto. She hesitantly responded. In a vice grip, he held her hand while she discretely winced in pain.

"A pleasure." Erichthonius moved closer to Alecto. "I've heard *everything* about you. I have several friends who cannot wait to see you in action at tonight's exhibition." It was a fair warning.

"Speaking of," Mona interjected. "I have an extra ticket! Would you like to go? It would be a delight if you could join us."

Still holding Alecto's crumpled hand in his own, the demigod said he'd love to.

CHAPTER 34
IN PLAIN SIGHT

AFTER BIDDING ATHENA GOODBYE, Hermes flew like lightning to the realm of Gaia. Time streaked behind him in straight lines with hardly a notice. When he got to the Getty Museum, the scantily-clad god looked for a spot in its central garden to hide.

In plain sight.

Well, it was definitely a better idea in the *classroom* than it was standing nearly naked in the sunshine of the outdoors. The Messenger God tiptoed the grounds until he found a place where the trees and shrubs surrounded him. Several times along the way, the god had to stop mid-movement when a human happened by. Once among the thick vegetation, Hermes was careful not to appear too interesting as to not attract too much attention from passersby. As he stood there, still as stone, he was certain he looked as ridiculous as he felt.

If that reveler Dionysus, the God of Wine, could see me now, he wouldn't need his strong drink for a good laugh.

Hermes could see it now. He'd be the laughingstock of the Pantheon.

Getting inside the museum was easy. As the building was closing for the evening, Hermes snuck in through a loading dock door and flew down the hallways to the Exhibitions Pavilion. His speed made him little more than a blur to human eyes and a breeze against their skin. He flew past museum-goers, ruffling their hair, papers, and dresses in his wake and causing them to eye one another suspiciously.

The pavilion housing *The Ancients Alive* exhibition was closed to the public and wouldn't be opened until tonight's preview party. Hermes crept inside and cased the dark room. If he were the sentimental type, he would've been homesick. There were vases and urns formerly used in the temples during worship that he had not seen in years. Bronze coins depicting fellow gods and nymphs alike were displayed in glass cases. He laughed aloud at some of the busts of Greek heroes with their heroism grossly exaggerated in their features. Vice-like jaws. Jutting chins. Strong brows. People have always needed their heroes to look like something other than the faces in their very own mirrors. That way, it's always someone else's obligation to be brave.

But then, there was Charis.

Hermes stood before the towering Farnese Heracles marble statue and smiled. Given the demigod's legendary antics, he well understood the infatuation man had with Heracles.

But, enough of this reminiscing.

Hermes was not here for a stroll down memory lane.

He proceeded through the rooms of the exhibition. No jar. Perhaps it was still in storage and undetected. As he floated farther, he heard a door open behind him. His eyes darted back and forth. He quickly spied a chamber within the exhibition that displayed big marble and bronze statues. Hermes hid among them and stood very, very still.

"Put the pedestal in the back, there … " a short, round man instructed his struggling taller, leaner counterpart.

"The information label should already be hung on the wall. You'll find it."

His partner grunted his response and walked on, carrying the heavy ivory-colored pedestal. The rotund man walked the flow of the exhibition, tablet in hand. One by one, he checked things off his list. At some items, he typed frantic notes with the surprising speed of just one finger. At others, he simply said "uh huh" and moved on.

As he approached the room where Hermes stood, the god was certain of a premature discovery.

This could be a problem.

The checklist man continued his checking, getting closer and closer to the magnificent marble-like statue he'd never even noticed before.

By Zeus, this cannot be happening.

As he approached Hermes, a loud crash and louder cursing emitted from up the hall.

"Carl?" the checklist man called, wobbling in the direction of the commotion. "What's goin' on back there?"

A few minutes later, the two men walked past Hermes and toward the exit doors.

"It's a good thing that was only the glass, buddy," said the checklist man, slapping good ol' clumsy Carl on the back. "I've heard the jar that's going under it is a doozy. They don't know if that thing is real or not, but some say it could be Pandora's Jar."

The Fates—those odd, cunning sisters— had smiled upon Hermes.

CHAPTER 35
A NIGHT TO REMEMBER

Five or six huge searchlights fanned their beams across the cool December night sky over the Getty as the city of Los Angeles twinkled below. This was the largest Greek antiquities exhibition ever outside of Europe and the museum was lit up like the big deal it was. Shiny, black limousines lined the parking spaces and smartly dressed men and women rode the tram up to the center.

Charis, her family, and Gabe waited at the entrance for Mr. P. She watched as her mom fussed over Presley's tie.

"You look good, baby," Mona doted.

"Thanks, Mom," he smiled and gently grabbed her busy hands. She was dangerously close to embarrassing him.

"Do you mind if Nia and I go on inside?"

Presley had decided to bring a "date" to the event. Before picking her up, he gave his family stern instructions about not making a big deal about the pretty brown girl in the stunning green dress that stood beside him holding his hand.

"No, not at all. You two go on ahead, we'll catch up with you inside." Presley grimaced. "Or not. Geesh. Have fun." Charis made googly eyes at him before he and his politely ignored date left.

"She's so pretty," Charis finally admitted now that Presley was gone.

Mona turned her attention to Charis.

"She is. And so are you, baby girl." Mona took a look at Charis. She was a doll in her pink dress ... but those pink Keds.

"I still think your cute silver flats were a more obvious choice."

As Charis thought about what her night might have in store, she imagined running could be a part of it. She didn't want to chance it with leather-soled shoes, so ...

"Charis," Mr. P called. He shuffled his way over to her and greeted everyone.

"Mom? Dad? Do you mind if we hang with Mr. P tonight?" Charis pressed her palms together as she made pleading eyes at them. "He's promised to tell us everything he knows about the pieces inside."

Mona looked around at the crowd of people streaming up the stairs to the entrance hall and then back at her puppy-eyed daughter. She was so cute. Plus, this was the happiest she'd seen Charis since her falling apart at the breakfast table and storming out the door.

"There are a lot of people coming tonight and I want you two safe. You can go with Mr. Papadakis if you promise to stay together and not to leave his side," she responded.

"We promise!" Charis and Gabe said together.

"Thank you, Mr. Papadakis," Mona smiled. "You're actually doing all of us a big favor."

Mona heard someone call her name from far away.

"I've got a lot of schmoozing to do and people to please. I know these two will have a much better time with you tonight than they would with Evan and me."

"Mona," Richard called again as he came running down the entry stairs.

"You two behave yourselves and have a ball."

"Thanks, Mom. Bye Dad!" Charis said as she walked away.

Richard approached Mona and Evan, out of breath.

"Mona." He had a worried look on his face. "I can't find Mr. Ecto."

"What?" Mona said, but not too loudly. She didn't want to attract any more attention than Richard had in running down the stairs. "What do you mean?" Mona asked out of politeness.

In truth, Mona didn't really care. Her responsibility for Mr. Ecto was finished. Between the dinner debacle and her awkward experience with him at today's play, she'd had quite enough of the strange man from Greece. But the look of panic on Richard's face moved her. He looked desperate.

"Honey," she said turning to Evan. "Do you mind if I help Richard look for Mr. Ecto?"

"Of course not, babe," Evan assured. "Come and find me when you can. I'll be near the food." He kissed her on the cheek before she turned and disappeared among the other guests going up the stairs.

* * *

She was done. No more charades. No more pretending. This human experiment had reached its brutal end. She was tired of their incessant talking. She was sick of fumbling around with the makeshift human body she wore. She just wanted to get the jar and go home.

Alecto crouched in an empty storage room waiting for her sisters to come. The Erinyes Sisters were among the few creatures who could travel seamlessly, magically from one realm to the other. It made sense. They frequently accompanied their victims from the earth to the Underworld, and were often the reasons behind the transition from life to the afterlife in the first place.

Life. Afterlife.

She couldn't wait to get back to the business of torturing the deserving. She had been tortured here on Gaia long enough.

Alecto seized the first opportunity that presented itself to slip away from that Richard Burnett fellow. They'd have to figure this evening out without her. Not that it mattered. What did she care about these humans? The jar. She just wanted to get that blasted jar.

Alecto opened and closed the hand that Erichthonius clinched in his grip earlier at the play. It still smarted. If she could, she'd make him pay for that.

She looked up, noticing that the room got warmer and the dark got darker. In a puff of soot and ash, Tisiphone and Megaera appeared.

Alecto stood up, her small mouth upturned in a painful looking smile. She beheld her sisters in all of their horrific glory—black wings, red eyes, and terrible, gray countenances. Without a moment's hesitation, Alecto shrugged off the human facade she'd grown sick of wearing. She was, at last, her horrible self.

The three Erinyes Sisters stood in a circle looking and grinning at one another. The snakes upon their heads writhed and wiggled a dark dance of reunion. The three Underworld monsters began a low, menacing cackle. There was trouble afoot, and they were going to be at the center of it.

*   *   *

There was no fashionably late with this crowd. The exhibition hadn't been open for ten minutes before guests poured into the entrance hall. There were smiling people and photographers everywhere. The poster images that had sprung up all over the city of LA weeks ago were now displayed on stanchion signs in the brightly lit building.

They read "*The Ancients Alive*" and featured the sculpted faces of one Greek god or another. Charis didn't know about Zeus (she hadn't met him yet ... and didn't know if she wanted to), but they had Athena all wrong. She was much prettier in real life.

Charis opened her little pink purse and took Nike out. She clasped the little goddess to the strap.

"Okay, now what do we do?" Charis asked of anyone who had a suggestion.

"I say we get this over with," said Gabe. "Let's find the stupid jar, open it, and then get the heck out of here. I'll say I got a stomach ache or something."

"Patience," Mr. P cautioned. Charis was so glad her mom had that extra ticket. She felt better with him here already.

"The jar could be anywhere. For all we know it might not even be displayed. It might still be in the storage room where I originally left it. In fact, I hope that's the case."

"It's not," Gabe said.

"What? How do you know?" Charis asked.

Gabe pointed his finger and Charis and Mr. P followed it to a large, glossy poster. On it was a picture of Pandora's Jar. The words 'New Arrival' were splashed across it like a banner. The three of them walked toward it and stared.

"By Zeus," said Mr. P slowly.

Charis felt a fire light in her birthmark.

"What tha? Now what?" Charis asked. Nike started to glow a little brighter, so Charis pulled her closer to her ear.

"Let's walk through the exhibition so I can survey the jar's surroundings," Nike instructed. "Just behave normally."

Charis didn't tell her this, but she'd stopped knowing what normal was ever since the little goddess flew into her life.

The three of them walked through the growing crowd and bypassed the waiters serving quiche bites and pâté. There was only a smattering of people in the actual exhibition. It was still early in the evening, and most people had mingling to do. Once Charis and the others walked through the exhibition doors, they kept a very slow pace.

"There could be any number of obstacles we might encounter, so be on the lookout, even now," Mr. P warned.

By "obstacles" he meant Alecto, Hades, and other powers that be. Charis appreciated his more artful word choice however. They walked straight past many beautiful Greek treasures without so much as a second glance.

"Over here," Mr. P said.

They entered the room where Hermes stood. There was a small group of people standing in front of him, rifling through their exhibition programs in search of information on the incredibly life-like statute of Hermes, the Messenger God. Of course, they would find none. Hermes looked annoyed.

"We've got to get rid of those people," Charis said.

Before she even finished her thought, Gabe walked over to the group and placed himself smack dab in the middle. Standing there in his smart, black suit with his hair actually combed and in place, Gabe let out a loud, long, putrid fart. Charis doubled over, laughing. The people standing around her stupidly grinning friend didn't think it was funny at all. Gasps of disgust rose up along with Gabe's offending smell. The group quickly dispersed and left them alone with Hermes.

"Well done, my little friend," Hermes said to Gabe through his barely moving mouth. "A gloriously executed plan."

"Sorry about that," Gabe smiled. "I didn't know what else to do. You're not supposed to yell fire in public places."

"You're not supposed to fart like that either," laughed Charis, walking toward them. Mr. P shook his head. When the tittering was over, Hermes returned to the business at hand.

"The jar, my friends, is just up that hall there," he said. His words were the calm before a storm.

"From what I gather, it is covered in glass and is the surprising star of this exhibition. They only placed it in the case moments ago and already its reputation of beauty grows. I have very little doubt that as more people arrive, there will be more crowding around it."

Nike glowed again and Charis lifted her once more to her ear.

"She says that we should attempt it now or at the very end of the evening when the crowds are thinner. But, there is no way of knowing how late my parents will stay," Charis said.

A threesome of hungry-eyed women walked toward the nearly nude Hermes to admire him but moved on when they saw that Charis and her group wouldn't budge.

"Go to it now to gauge its access," Hermes said. "If there is no one around, I will simply snatch it and meet up with you later so that you might fulfill your destiny."

"There are cameras," Gabe said, looking discretely overhead.

"They won't see him," Mr. P said. "He's too fast."

"Okay," Charis agreed. "We'll be right back. Don't you worry."

"Hurry," Hermes said, steeling himself as another group of gawkers came to appreciate him. Hermes loved being admired, but this was ridiculous.

*   *   *

The gallery talk was scheduled in five minutes. Richard and Mona searched the Getty's grounds high and low and there was no sign of Mr. Ecto. They climbed every single staircase the Getty had, searched through the crowds listening to music in the courtyard, and wandered both of its gardens with no luck. Mona sat near the entrance and rubbed her throbbing feet, unconcerned with who saw.

"I'm sorry, Richard," she groaned. "But, the evening has started and the show must go on."

Richard knew she was right, but boy, was he angry. He tried to remember who had recommended Mr. Ecto so that he could scold him or her later.

"You can do the talk yourself, Richard. Or maybe one of the other curators."

"I know. I know," he said, exasperated. "But, the truth is, as strange a man as Mr. Ecto is, he really knows his Greek antiquities. When we got around to talking shop, he was impressive. During our walkthrough yesterday, you should have heard him, Mona. He knew more about each object than I'd ever read in a book. He was masterful. I can only imagine what he would have said about that new jar we found." He sighed. "Oh well."

"There you are!" Evan said. "I've been looking all over for you. You okay?" It was unusual to see his wife out in the public massaging her bare foot while sitting in a semi-formal dress. He could tell she was already tired and the evening had only just begun.

"I am, babe. Thank you." She slipped her shoe back on. "Mr. Ecto is still missing, but our ever-professional host here is going to do an incredible job in his place. Right?"

Richard scratched his baldhead. "Sure, why not? Right."

*   *   *

There it was, in all of its glory. Charis circled the pedestal and peered at the jar inside. If people couldn't tell with one glance that it was the real deal, then they couldn't see that the sky was blue.

"Look at it," she said in wonder. "It's beautiful." Charis reached out to touch the glass. The surface was hot beneath her fingertips, just like the birthmark between her shoulder blades.

"And, deadly," Mr. P whispered. "Let us not forget, this jar is the source of great trouble. Not only yours, Charis, but that of the whole world." He bent down and looked at the relief of Zeus giving the jar to Pandora.

"Still, Hope remains. Just inside." Mr. P's eyes glistened as he thought of Elpis alone in the jar when she was so desperately needed within the earth.

An elderly couple joined them at the jar.

"Isn't that something?" the husband said to the wife.

"It's just lovely," she said. "I hope they can authenticate it soon. The art world would have acquired a great boon." Charis looked behind her. There were more people coming their way to see the newly acclaimed masterpiece. At this rate, they'd never get a chance to open it.

"Ladies and gentlemen," a pleasant female voice traveled through the museum speakers. "Please join Mr. Knox Wentworth, CEO of the Getty Trust, and Mr. Richard Burnett, Director of Exhibitions and Public Programs of the Getty Center, in the Entrance Hall as we welcome you to *The Ancients Alive*."

Docents guided everyone toward the front of the museum where a crowd was gathering. The band stopped playing, food service was suspended, and the lights were dimmed in the exhibition area to encourage everyone's attendance. As Charis and the others filed out of the Exhibition Pavilion, passing a motionless Hermes along the way, they knew this was the best opportunity they might have all night to get the jar.

"Stay on the outside of the crowd," Mr. P instructed. "We'll slip away and meet Hermes at the case. There'll be no need to wait. You can open the jar here, and that'll be that." Charis reached back with sweaty palms to rub her itching birthmark.

*   *   *

They were not the only ones to hear the announcement and, thus, the opportunity. Holding claw-like hands in a circle, Alecto and her sisters vanished into thin air and turned into smoke and ash. Only their red eyes remained as they were. From the storage room where they hid, their thick, black smoke drifted beneath the door and down the hallways of the Getty. They stayed close to walls and corners, nooks and crannies, as they drifted swiftly toward Pandora's Jar. They blew through the crowd of people and into the Exhibitions Pavilion. There, they hovered in a darkened corner and became a part of it, unseen. The Erinyes Sisters were nothing more than a billow of smoke with blood-red eyes peering out from within.

Disembodied voices spoke to one another.

"We must search discretely," Megaera said. "Discretely search for the jar."

The smoky sisters blew from one painting and into another, hiding their ashen bodies within ancient, black brushstrokes.

"Do you sssee it?" hissed Alecto, her red eyes darting back and forth.

"Do you see it?" hissed Tisiphone.

Through the air, nothing more than particles, they wafted onto The Wedding of Thetis pyxis and found refuge in its ebony finish.

"Do you see it?" hissed Megaera

"Shh," answered Alecto. "Sssomeone comes."

The sisters shut their red eyes to remain unseen. A security guard strolled into the room, making his rounds. When he reached the Greek exhibition, he started to feel terribly uneasy. Queasy even. He walked a little farther into the room and stood next to the vase into which the Erinyes Sisters had disappeared. A foul smell permeated the room. Overcome with nausea, the guard cupped his mouth as the bile in his stomach leapt and rose, burning his throat. He couldn't get out of there fast enough as he ran to find a bathroom.

"Go," Tisiphone urged, when they were sure the guard was gone.

The Erinyes Sisters floated deeper into the exhibition and closer to Hermes, unaware of the watching Messenger God.

*   *   *

"We are so delighted that you've chosen to be with us on this preview night of our biggest exhibition to date, *The Ancients Alive*." There was a round of applause as Richard began his unplanned speech.

"In partnership with the British Museum, we are proud to present rarely-seen pieces of Greek antiquity from all corners of the world ..."

Charis made sure that her mom, dad, Presley, and his non-date Nia saw her. In part, because she thought it would keep them from coming to look for her later. But also, because there might not be any "later." Charis knew that this could be her last time seeing her family. Ever.

Somewhere in the building, there were others who wanted the jar too—others willing to do anything to keep Charis from it. Try as she might not to think about that, she knew that she could very well die tonight. The terror Charis experienced as she drowned beneath Hades's rain seized her again. Once the speech started, she and the rest pulled away from the crowd and stealthily ran toward the Exhibition Pavilion, but not before Charis turned to look at her family a final time.

"Hermes," Mr. P called as they entered.

The Erinyes Sisters stopped their searching, mid-air. Suspended in the middle of the room like that, they looked like a low flying storm cloud.

"Hermesss?" Alecto whispered.

The three sisters darted into the folds of fabric on a massive sculpture nearby and hid in the shadows of its skirt.

To the surprise of Charis and the others, Hermes remained quiet. Nike's body began to tingle and glow.

"There's a reason he doesn't answer," the goddess said. "Something is wrong."

She unhooked herself from Charis's purse and flew to the front of the group, sword drawn.

Hermes looked down at his skirt where the hellish Erinyes Sisters had unwittingly taken refuge and hid.

Can I wrap them up and capture them? How does this work? Can they travel their smoky bodies through my clothes or can they be trapped and contained?

* * *

"Our organization is deeply grateful to you, our community. Your help has enabled this global effort and has paved the way for future ones to come. Not only for this museum, but for museums around the world ..."

* * *

Nike inched forward in the darkness until she could see Hermes from a distance. She shined her light, green, a little brighter. Nike's light caught Hermes's eyes that had been trained on the sisters. It also caught the attention of the Erinyes Sisters. When Hermes looked back down at his skirt where the three hideous sisters were, he saw three pairs of blood-red eyes peering back up at him from the shadows.

In a blur of movement, a wrinkle in time, Hermes wrapped his draping clothes around the sisters, hoping to capture them. He didn't. Between the fibers of the cloth, smoke pushed through and formed three horrific figures standing at the ready in the middle of the room.

Nike charged without a word. Alecto retreated and ran toward the vase. Having only recently tasted the little goddess's sword, she wanted no part of it so she left her sisters to fight. They could handle it. Megaera flapped her black wings and took to the air toward the little goddess, but Nike was too quick and small. She flew beneath the winged Megaera like a flash and grabbed her toes, yanking her hard to the ground. The glass cases shook around them. Charis and Gabe hid behind Mr. P and watched the fighting in shock.

Hermes left his pedestal and took flight to pursue the fleeting Alecto.

She must not get the jar.

He overtook her easily, but as he reached to grab her, she became black dust in his arms. No matter. He'd get the jar and give it to the girl.

* * *

"I'd especially like to thank our incredible, flexible team here at the Getty," Richard added. "In case you are one of the few who have not yet heard, we've only recently acquired a most perplexing, intriguing, and delightful item …"

* * *

Hermes stood his ground before the jar, ready to defend it against further attacks, but then a scream lifted … a scream from Charis. Tisiphone had charged Charis, Gabe, and Mr. P. Unexpectedly, Mr. P dropped to the ground and slithered toward the approaching Erinyes Sister faster than Charis or Gabe had ever seen him walk. Tisiphone and Mr. P had one another in their grips. Snakes hissed and spat as they battled. Gabe grabbed Charis's hand.

"Run!" he yelled, dragging her past the fighting gods and toward the jar. "Run to the jar!"

* * *

"We've named it Pandora's Jar because, while there is much about it that remains a mystery, the relief clearly depicts the myth of Pandora ..."

* * *

Hermes flew toward the kids who were running toward him, ready to scoop them up. Gabe suddenly fell hard to the ground and was being dragged from behind. It was Alecto. She clutched Gabe's ankle firmly in her hand. He kicked and tried to free himself.

"No!" Charis screamed, turning around to rescue her friend.

"Stay there, Charis," Hermes yelled in shock waves as he flew past her. In no time, he was back with the boy in one arm and picking her up in the other.

"I've got you two, don't worry." His eyes were calm. His words were, too.

The world was a blur within Hermes's speed. Charis could hardly lift her head against the wind. The jar was just ahead, but so was Alecto, standing right beside it.

"Look!" shouted Gabe. Alecto turned into black mist and blew beneath the glass. She surrounded the jar in her ash.

* * *

"It was clearly done by a master, and you don't need to be an expert to reach that conclusion. The amount of detail, especially in the faces, is staggering on such a small surface ..."

*   *   *

From the inside out, Alecto toppled the glass, setting off a silent alarm. Both the jar and Alecto's thick smoke began to vanish and fade away. Nike flew into the black mist, darting in and out of it. The little goddess was a whirlwind, flying around and around scattering the particles of Alecto in every direction until the monster could no longer hold herself together.

The jar dropped to the floor and rolled toward Charis. Hermes set her down beside it.

"Open it!" he yelled. "Open it, quickly."

Charis grabbed the jar. Its white marble turned bright blue as it nearly jumped from her hands. The jar vibrated wildly at Charis's touch. Charis twisted the lid, gritting her teeth. It didn't budge. Her hands were sweaty with nerves.

"Ugh!" she grunted.

She twisted hard again and it started to give. Charis almost had it opened when the thick black soot of the three Erinyes Sisters surrounded her. Startled, Charis dropped the jar to the floor and was unable to find it through all the smoke. On all fours, Charis felt around in the dark for the jar, gagging and coughing in the Erinyes Sisters's soot.

"Help," she choked. "Somebody help me!" Charis swatted away the ash all around her. "Help! Nike! Hermes!"

The hot breath of her would-be murderer warmed Charis's ears.

"You're coming with *me*, Charisss!" Alecto snarled from within the darkness.

Charis couldn't breathe. She couldn't see. Pressure closed in on her every side. Her body lifted from the ground and twisted and turned in the air. Her hair whipped all around her in the tornado of the Erinyes Sisters. She saw nothing but blackness, with her and the jar suspended in the middle of it. Gabe screamed her name from somewhere far away.

If I could just get the jar.

Nike tried to disperse the Erinyes's smoke once more. But there were three sisters this time, and she was too small against their current.

Then Hermes pressed through the darkness and reached for Charis's hand, but he missed. She was traveling. Away. She didn't know where she was going or where they were taking her, but she feared the worst.

Alerted by the silent alarm triggered by Alecto, several security guards rushed past the crowd listening to Richard's speech and headed toward the Exhibitions Pavilion.

*   *   *

"Well, enough talking from me," Richard said. "Thank you, again, for your contribution toward the success of this groundbreaking exhibition."

*   *   *

Hermes reached again. This time, he grabbed Charis by the ankles as the force of the wind tugged her in the opposite direction. She only saw him in the black mist from the waist up.

"The jar," he yelled to Nike behind him. "Can you stop the jar from being sucked in?"

Nike whizzed past Charis. The little goddess flew in front of the moving jar and tried to stop it from getting pulled closer to the away place. She strained against the wind with all of her might to push the jar to Charis.

"Can you reach it, Charis?" Nike yelled over the blowing black wind. "Can you open it?"

The girl stretched her arms and Nike pushed her hardest but Charis couldn't reach it. In her stretching, Charis slipped from Hermes's hands. She flew loose and untethered, helpless in the whipping black smoke. As she spun into the darkness, her wild limbs knocked Nike from the jar and sent her flying. Charis and the jar went tumbling into the long, black tube of nothingness that she thought would finally end at the place of her death.

Athena. ATHENA! Along with Athena, move also your hand.

Charis decided she wasn't going to helplessly drift in the middle of the Erinyes Sisters's blackness toward her doom without a struggle. She would fight. She would fight to get the jar. She would fight to get back home.

"Charis, no!" Nike shouted as she saw Charis kicking her legs and trying to catch up to the spinning jar ahead of her. "No! Stay put. We're coming!"

Charis moved her arms as if she were swimming and got closer to the jar.

The world. The world is counting on me. Mom. Dad. Presley.

She grazed the jar with her outstretched fingers.

Depending on me …

Just a little farther … she had it!

* * *

"We invite you to enjoy the food prepared right here in our very own world-class restaurant. Enjoy the beautiful classical music played by members of the Santa Monica Orchestra. And, most of all, enjoy the art, courtesy of the great Greek artists of the past."

* * *

The security guards, four of them, reached the pavilion. As they entered the room, the smoke coming from inside it caused them to retch and gag. Their burning eyes sent them running out of the room in tears. It didn't smell like a fire, but it sure felt like one.

"Sound the fire alarm," the leader instructed.

Another guard went running.

* * *

Charis swung toward Nike with the jar in her hands. She was so far away. The girl wrestled against the black wind, her eyes watered against the force. She kicked her way toward Nike, clutching the jar tightly to her chest. She had to get out. Nike flew fast toward Charis. When she reached her, the little goddess tugged at her dress collar, pulling her along. But they made only slow progress. Charis looked up and saw Hermes ahead flying toward them. She breathed a sigh of relief. It was going to be all right. They were going to make it.

*   *   *

An alarm sounded in the museum and nervous chattering passed through the crowd. The same pleasant-voiced woman spoke again through the museum speakers.

"Please evacuate the building at the nearest exit. This is not a test. Please evacuate the building at the nearest exit. This is not a test."

The crowd scrambled in a panic. Mona looked around and saw everyone but Charis and Gabe. The crowd shoved her back and toward the doors as she tried to go against it in search of her daughter. She felt a hand. It was Evan. He grabbed her and pulled her back.

"Evan! I don't see Charis. I don't see our baby."

"Go outside, honey," he yelled, steering her towards the exit. "I'll find her. I promise."

Mona was swallowed in the surging flood of people and pushed out of the entrance doors.

*   *   *

When Hermes reached Charis and Nike, the world around them became perfectly still. All went calm and quiet. All went away. They were in nothing and nowhere. Charis knew this feeling. She'd had it whenever the gods met with one another. It was that feeling of not time and not space. It could only mean one thing. Or one person. Hades. Hades was here.

Charis saw the gray god smirking in front of her with Gabe painfully struggling in his arms. The smoke that, only moments ago, had suffocated and abused Charis vanished and she fell hard to the ground. The Erinyes Sisters must have retreated in fear.

"Give me the jar," Hades calmly demanded.

"Don't do it, Charis," Gabe shouted through gasps. "Don't do it."

She looked at Nike and Hermes and they both nodded yes. They would deal with the God of the Underworld later. For now, they just wanted everyone safe.

Charis moved closer to Hades. "Let him go first," she said, surprised by how calm she sounded.

"You make demands of me?" Hades hugged Gabe's waist tighter and caused him to cry out in pain. The Underworld God dug his fingernails into the flesh of Gabe's side.

"Please. Please let him go or ..." Charis looked around. " ... or I will open the jar. I promise. I will." She gripped the lid in her hands.

"If you do, I will kill him. I will. Now, come closer," Hades snarled. Charis took a few steps. "Closer!" Hades yelled. "There. That's good." Hades threw Gabe to the ground, where he landed with a thud, and placed his heavy foot on the boy's back. Just in case. "Now bring the jar to me, *girl*" he growled.

Charis carefully approached Hades. She looked down at Gabe beneath the god's foot. He looked ashamed as tears streamed down his cheeks.

"I'm sorry, Charis," he cried.

Charis didn't want to hand over the jar to Hades, but she knew she must. Using extreme caution, she extended the jar toward the god. He briefly smiled at her. As Hades took the jar in his massive hands, he took hold of Charis's hand too.

Away. They traveled, went, dove, jumped, ran, fell away. She fought to free herself, but the god was so strong. She beat his chest with her free hand, but he was made of rock. She kicked his legs, but they were steel. She finally bit down as hard as she could on his hand and he, for a split second, released her.

Charis scrambled to her feet. She took off running on top of the gray nowhere, away from Hades. He pursued her, gaining ground with every step. Charis saw a light ahead that she knew would lead back to her world, to Hermes, to Nike, to Gabe, to her family, and to school dances where she would wear new dresses and her hair up in a messy but stylish knot. Charis ran on, but Hades ran faster.

* * *

Evan pushed through the crowd looking for his daughter. He would try the exhibition room if he could just reach it.

"Sir," a security guard grabbed him by the arm. "Sir, you can't stay here. You have to leave the building."

"But, my daughter. She's inside," he insisted.

"Sir!"

Evan pulled free of the guard's grip and kept pushing his way through the frenzied crowd.

* * *

It's not supposed to end this way. I'm supposed to save the world.

Charis was exhausted and Hades continued after her, his every footstep a threat.

The prophecy. What about the prophecy?

Charis labored to lift each foot as she ran. She didn't think she could go on. She stumbled forward, nearly falling.

What about all that "chosen" stuff? What about my Mark of Hermes? What about my ... my wings?

In a burst of bright light, in a gust of wind, Charis Parks, Child of Grace and hope for her world, whiffed off of her feet and jerked clumsily into the air.

"My wings," she sobbed, stunned and breathless.

Charis flip-flapped her wings and flew through the air in herky, jerky movements. She soared up and away from the God of the Underworld, growing faster with every beat. Hades stood beneath her, shaking his fist with a look of surprise and hatred. Charis and her silver, feathered wings kept right on flying toward the light, wildly spinning toward home, free. She would escape. She would cheat fate, this time. She would live.

Charis spilled into the light and landed exactly where she had left the room with the Erinyes Sisters an eternity ago.

"You did it!" Gabe said. "You made it!" Gabe hugged her neck tightly. Hermes kissed her furrowed forehead and showered her with praise. Nike glowed all manner of colors before her, displaying the joy that words never could. Mr. P lifted her chin and told her how proud he was of her.

Overjoyed, Charis embraced them all within her brilliant, shining wings before her body, wracked with the trauma it had just survived, started to shake uncontrollably.

"Charis?" Hermes said, concern bathing his voice. "Charis? Are you all right? What's the matter, dear one?"

Shivering, Charis looked up at her friends, bewildered and beaten.

"The jar. What about the jar?" she asked before she fainted.

SATURDAY

*Hope is the only good that is common to all men; those
who have nothing else possess hope still.*

—THALES

CHAPTER 36
HOPE + LESS =

CHARIS WOKE UP in the UCLA Medical Center with the sun streaming into her beige and green room. Her mom, dad, brother, and best friend all sat around her bed, looking up at the TV. A news reporter was talking about last night's incident at the Getty. The Liam Hemsworth lookalike said that authorities were unsure about the cause of the harmless smoke that overcame many of the museum's guests. Charis lay there quietly and listened to the next story about a mall shooting in Oregon ... and the next about the spread of AIDS in Europe.

It was Charis's fault. Every ill, every sorrow, was her fault. Charis felt she was to blame for the sad state of the world. If only she had opened the jar.

A single tear ran from her eye, encouraged by the guilt flooding her heart.

She groaned as she tried to sit up and couldn't. Everything hurt.

"Hey there, sleepyhead." Evan said, gently. He held her hand in his. "Don't try to move, Sunny. Everything is okay. You're okay." She looked at her mom who had tears in her eyes.

"What happened?" Charis croaked. Her throat was dry and the sound of her own voice hurt her head.

"Someone thought there was a fire at the museum last night and everyone in the place panicked," her dad explained.

"But, after the firemen arrived, they couldn't find any evidence of a fire. There was just a faint, awful smell in the air. They couldn't tell where the smell came from, only that it wasn't dangerous."

Gabe and Charis exchanged a subtle glance.

"After all of the confusion subsided, I guess the party continued without another hitch. Except where you were concerned, love," Mona said, reaching out and stroking her daughter's cheek.

"Why am I here? I don't remember what …" Charis muttered.

Gabe stood up and spoke before anyone else could.

"We were running to get out of the building when you slipped and fell. You hit your head pretty hard on the floor. That's when I ran to get help and bumped into your dad in the hallway." Gabe winked his eye at her, but he didn't need to.

"The most important thing is that you're all right now," Mona said.

Presley walked over to his little sister and kissed her on the head. "I was worried about you, Sunny. Don't ever scare me like that again. I love you, sis."

"I love you too, Pres."

Charis felt so lucky to be surrounded by her family. She knew how close she'd come to never seeing them again, but her joy was short-lived as she remembered her failure with the jar. It broke her heart. She had let them down and they didn't even know it.

"Do you think I can have a moment alone with Gabe?" Charis asked.

"Sure, babe. We'll go grab some breakfast," Evan said. "Gabe, can we bring you back anything?"

"No thanks, Mr. Parks. I'm fine." Charis noticed that there wasn't a shred of nervousness in Gabe around her dad this time. She guessed that after surviving last night, he had nothing more to fear. From anyone.

When her family left the room, Charis asked Gabe what had really happened. He sat down in a chair beside her bed.

"Turns out, Hades was in the exhibition room the whole time. He was wearing that Helm of Darkness thing so we couldn't see him. Hermes thought that Hades might be hiding somewhere and that's why he stayed back to protect me just in case. But when he saw you and Nike struggling in the dark, he went in to help you. That's when Hades grabbed me. Mr. P tried to take him, but he was no match for that guy. Hades was just too big and strong. He flung

Mr. P away like a rag doll. Anyway, before we went through that weird black tunnel thing, Hades put a fake jar where Pandora's used to be, so no one would suspect anything. Hades has the jar with him now. If the other gods are ever going to get it back, they'll have to fight for it in his realm, not ours."

The idea of going back to the Underworld sent chills down Charis's back. Her back! She turned around to see her wings.

"What happened to them? They're gone."

"I don't know," Gabe answered. "They did this sparkly thing and vanished like some kind of dust or something when you passed out."

She looked at him, embarrassed. She was a freak.

"Your wings rocked, Charis," he said, seeing her cheeks redden. "You know they did."

Charis scooted up in her bed and moaned aloud. God, was she sore!

"So what now?" she asked. Gabe shrugged his shoulders. Although she knew the answer to her next question, she asked it anyway.

"Where are Nike and the others?"

"Gone. They left to go back to Mt. Olympus. They've got a lot to figure out now. Both Nike and Hermes are concerned about things escalating. They're worried about Zeus and what would happen if he finds out about Hades's involvement in all of this. They think it could mean a full-blown war between the gods and man. They're going to do everything in their power to avoid that." Gabe paused. He saw the tears forming in Charis's eyes.

"I'm sorry, Charis."

"Me too," she said with her lip quivering.

"Oh," he said, reaching into his jacket pocket. "Before I forget ... Nike wanted you to have this." Gabe handed her a small keychain. It was an exact replica of Nike as Charis first had met her. She wrapped her hand around it and held it to her heart.

Nike said that until I opened the jar, she'd have to stay this way ...

"I failed, Gabe," Charis cried. "I failed. I let them down. I let myself down." Her every sob pounded inside her aching head. "I let the world down!"

"It's okay. It's okay." Gabe held her hand. He didn't know what else to say or do.

* * *

The hospital released Charis later that morning. She was glad to be home, but it wasn't the same. She sat on the edge of her bed and stared at the lifeless, plastic Nike in her hands. Tears threatened to choke her again. Charis was tired and wanted to sleep so she crawled in bed, every movement causing her to wince in pain. As she laid her head on her pillow, the lingering smell of the Erinyes Sisters emanated from her curls and caused her to gag.

Charis got up and dragged herself to the bathroom for a long, hot shower. She stood beneath the water and let it wash away the remains of her night at the museum. When at last she stood before her mirror, she had no words of wisdom, encouragement, or anything else remotely positive to say. It was just all bad. She tried, and she failed.

She failed.

Charis found her word. It was easy, really. She groaned as she raised her arm to write.

"Failure."

It's what she was. It's how she felt. It's how the night ended. It was all one big failure. She lowered her eyes in shame, unable to look at herself in the blurry mirror any longer.

In the privacy of the bathroom, Charis allowed herself to cry the tears she'd kept bottled inside. She buried her face in her hands and sobbed so freely that she almost didn't hear the squeaking of writing on the mirror above her. Charis slowly lifted her tear-stained eyes, expecting to see a written warning from Hades, or worse, his scowl reflecting back at her.

Her word, "failure," had been wiped clean. In its place was a quote from Sophocles:

"Bear up, my child, bear up; Zeus who oversees and directs all things is still mighty in heaven."

A loud thunderbolt cracked through the fog of the mirror leaving an unmistakable signature:

Charis nearly jumped out of her skin.

"What tha?!"

Zeus! He knows!

Charis covered her mouth before she could scream. This changed everything.

Zeus knows!

Charis reached out toward the mirror, afraid to touch it. Her fingers hovered over the blazing signature, trembling. She leaned over her bathroom sink and peered into the foggy mirror, wide-eyed. She hoped, maybe, to see the King of the Gods. What she saw were flashing glimpses of her future within the mirror's glass instead. She saw a little Nike, wielding her trusted sword. She saw a brave Gabe standing by her side in battle. Hermes tore through the air and she soared beside him. There was a god, Poseidon likely, with his trident raised above his waves. There was Hades, surrounded by the Erinyes Sisters and legions more. And there was the jar. Charis saw it. It was in her hands.

There would be tears. Some would be lost, some betrayed, some forgotten. There would be victories. There might be blood. But there would also be Hope, and another chance for Charis to set her free into the world. She wouldn't blow it, not again.

"I'm bearing up, Zeus," Charis said, a smile finally finding her face. "Whatever the heck that means. I'm bearing up."

THE END

ACKNOWLEDGMENTS

I love Charis! I just do! So you can only imagine my gratitude for everyone who helped me bring her to life. I want to thank those friends and family members who read early and awful drafts of my manuscript that was filled with potential and little else. I appreciate your support, feedback, and belief. The folks who suffered through *one* or *every* sentence of Charis's beginnings are many, and they are (in no particular order): Lisa Joga, Candice Carr, Renee Aikens, Leroy Mitchell, Arlene Yoshida, Wyne Vu Cler, Dee Dee Bonifant, Meredith Keltz, Kanesha Baynard, Collinus Newsome Hutt, Jennifer Pierce, Tara Walters, Ryan Walters, Cole Walters, Barbara Joyner, Monique Ruffin, Alexis Robinson, Monique Conard Gafford, Jaya Gafford, (Faith Gafford too for good measure), Corey Portfolio, J.D Mason, Ann Engels Nogueira, Declan Ning, Journey Simmons, KT, Kaitlin McCarthy, Jessica Carter, and Charmaine Robles Velasco. I appreciate you. (And, if I've forgotten any of you, please forgive me, and let me take you to coffee.)

There were two lovely young ladies who served as gracious models for the Charis illustrated throughout this book. I'd like to thank my niece, Charis Conard, and my young friend Esmé DeCoster. Your inner and outer beauty inspires.

Thank you to my incredibly talented brother and illustrator, Vincent Andrew Conard. Not only did you support my vision, you helped illuminate it and gave it breath, beauty, and a soul. You're an amazing artist and I love you. That a picture is worth a thousand words has never been truer than what you expressed throughout the pages of this book. What do your students say as you draw? That you're a beast? Well, they're right!

To the entire team at Booktrope, thank you for creating such a vibrant environment where dreams can grow. The future of publishing is here, and you have led the way in ushering it in. I'm grateful to be a part of this wonderful, way-making community.

Finally, Dawn Pearson, thank you for being the perfect editor for this project and me. I mean it. Your gentle guidance, ultimate wisdom, keen eye, and sweet affection for Charis were a blessing—straight from the gods themselves.

And, speaking of God, thank you too.

MORE GREAT READS FROM BOOKTROPE

Moonlight and Oranges by **Elise Stephens** (Young Adult) Love, fate, a secret dream journal, a psychic's riddle, and a downright scary mother-of-the-beau. A timeless tale of youthful romance.

The Dirt by **Lori Culwell** (Young Adult) The beauty, the nerd, the tomboy and the missing sister. The wealthiest family has the darkest of secrets. But then, nobody's perfect!

The Printer's Devil by **Chico Kidd** (Historical Fantasy) A demon summoned long ago by a heartbroken lover in Cromwellian England, now reawakened by a curious scholarly researcher. Who will pay the price?

Billy Purgatory: I Am the Devil Bird by **Jesse James Freeman** (Fantasy) A sweet-talkin', bad-ass skateboarder battles devil birds, time zombies, and vampires while pursuing Anastasia, the girl of his dreams (and they aren't all nightmares).

Demon Weather (Da Silva Tales, #1) by **Chico Kidd** (Fantasy) The adventures of Captain Da Silva, who has lost an eye and gained the power to see ghosts. A rollicking, rip-roaring read.

The Chosen (Book One of the Portals of Destiny Series) by **Shay West** (Fantasy) To each of the four planets are sent four Guardians, with one mission: to protect and serve the Chosen, those who alone can save the galaxy from the terrifying Meekon. An epic story of life throughout the galaxy, and the common purpose that brings them together.

… and many more!

Sample our books at:
www.booktrope.com

Learn more about our new approach to publishing at:
www.booktropepublishing.com

CPSIA information can be obtained at www.ICGtesting.com
Printed in the USA
BVOW040547160513

320849BV00001B/2/P